I0702829

Hawk on the Hunt is a work of fiction. Names, characters, places, and incidents are the products of the author's imagination and are used fictitiously. Any resemblance to actual events, locales, or persons, living or dead, is entirely coincidental.

Copyright © 2024 by Tina Folsom

All rights reserved.

Published in the United States

Cover design: Leah Kaye Suttle

Author Photo: © Marti Corn Photography

Printed in the United States of America

BOOKS BY TINA FOLSOM

Ace on the Run (Code Name Stargate, Book 1)

Fox in plain Sight (Code Name Stargate, Book 2)

Yankee in the Wind (Code Name Stargate, Book 3)

Tiger on the Prowl (Code Name Stargate, Book 4)

Hawk on the Hunt (Code Name Stargate, Book 5)

Samson's Lovely Mortal (Scanguards Vampires, Book 1)

Amaury's Hellion (Scanguards Vampires, Book 2)

Gabriel's Mate (Scanguards Vampires, Book 3)

Yvette's Haven (Scanguards Vampires, Book 4)

Zane's Redemption (Scanguards Vampires, Book 5)

Quinn's Undying Rose (Scanguards Vampires, Book 6)

Oliver's Hunger (Scanguards Vampires, Book 7)

Thomas's Choice (Scanguards Vampires, Book 8)

Silent Bite (Scanguards Vampires, Book 8 1/2)

Cain's Identity (Scanguards Vampires, Book 9)

Luther's Return (Scanguards Vampires, Book 10)

Blake's Pursuit (Scanguards Vampires, Book 11)

Fateful Reunion (Scanguards Vampires, Book 11 1/2)

John's Yearning (Scanguards Vampires, Book 12)

Ryder's Storm (Scanguards Vampires, Book 13)

Damian's Conquest (Scanguards Vampires, Book 14)

Grayson's Challenge (Scanguards Vampires, Book 15)

Isabelle's Forbidden Love (Scanguards Vampires Book 16)

Cooper's Passion (Scanguards Vampires, Book 17)

Lover Uncloaked (Stealth Guardians, Book 1)

Master Unchained (Stealth Guardians, Book 2)

Warrior Unraveled (Stealth Guardians, Book 3)

Guardian Undone (Stealth Guardians, Book 4)

Immortal Unveiled (Stealth Guardians, Book 5)

Protector Unmatched (Stealth Guardians, Book 6)

Demon Unleashed (Stealth Guardians, Book 7)

A Touch of Greek (Out of Olympus, Book 1)

A Scent of Greek (Out of Olympus, Book 2)

A Taste of Greek (Out of Olympus, Book 3)

A Hush of Greek (Out of Olympus, Book 4)

Venice Vampyr (Novellas 1 – 4)

Teasing (The Hamptons Bachelor Club, Book 1)

Enticing (The Hamptons Bachelor Club, Book 2)

Beguiling (The Hamptons Bachelor Club, Book 3)

Scorching (The Hamptons Bachelor Club, Book 4)

Alluring (The Hamptons Bachelor Club, Book 5)

Sizzling (The Hamptons Bachelor Club, Book 6)

Reversal of Fate (Time Quest, Book 1)

Harbinger of Destiny (Time Quest, Book 2)

HAWK ON THE HUNT

CODE NAME STARGATE #5

TINA FOLSOM

1

With his back to the three-story building, Dylan Steele sat down at one of the café's outdoor tables. It wasn't busy. From here, he could see everybody entering and leaving the coffee shop that was open until early evening. It was getting dark, and the air felt muggy like during most of the summer months in Washington D.C. Even though it was still mid-June, and the temperatures hadn't quite risen to the unbearable heat common in August, Dylan felt rivulets of sweat run down his back, making his casual shirt stick to his skin. He wasn't used to this humidity anymore. He'd spent the last four years in the cooler climate of the Pacific Northwest and along the Canadian border, hiding from his enemies. However, circumstances had demanded that he come back to Washington D.C., back to the place where it had all begun, and where it had to end. Once and for all.

Dylan sipped his iced coffee, before setting the plastic cup back on the round bistro table. A tealight candle sitting in a glass bowl filled with multi-colored glass pebbles cast abstract figures that danced in rhythm with the flickering flame on the table. Dylan merely pretended to look at the candle, when in reality he let his eyes roam without moving his head, without giving away that he was watching his surroundings like a hawk. Assessing, analyzing, always alert.

Maybe his watchful eye was the reason he'd been given the code name Hawk. And while the CIA program he'd once been part of didn't exist anymore, he was still Hawk, and he would always have to be vigilant like a hawk if he wanted to survive. The Stargate program was no more, but that didn't mean that his enemies had vanished too. His enemy could be sitting at one of the other bistro tables, or inside the café, or perhaps across the street in a parked car, watching him, waiting for the best opportunity to strike.

He'd never been one to give into paranoia, but he knew when to keep his guard up. Maybe coming here was a trap, but he had to take the risk. He also knew that his survival hinged on whether the person meeting him here tonight was friend or foe. Trust didn't come easy for him, but he would have to trust his gut once more, and hope that the instincts that had kept him alive for the last four years were still as sharp as ever. He crossed his fingers that the years away from D.C. hadn't made him negligent, because one moment of distraction could mean death.

From the corner of his eye, Dylan saw a man exit the café, a cup of coffee and a piece of pastry in his hands. The guy had entered the café three minutes earlier. Without hesitation, the stranger who looked to be in his mid to late thirties, walked toward him, put his purchased items on the bistro table, and sat down with such confidence that a casual observer would assume they met at the same table every day.

"Hey," the man with the dark hair and the five o'clock shadow said. "How've you been?"

Dylan gave a curt nod, while his nape prickled with awareness. "And you?"

"Same." The stranger took a sip from his coffee, before adding, "Ever seen the movie Zulu? Michael Caine starred in it."

There it was: the message to identify him as the man he was supposed to meet. Not that it was necessary. The prickling sensation on his nape had already identified the stranger. Dylan had first felt that same sensation when he'd met Henry Sheppard, the man who'd recruited him into the top-secret CIA program, in person. It had been a revelation.

"I saw Zulu only a few days ago," Dylan replied, though he wasn't talking about the movie, but the man whose code name was Zulu. Zulu was the reason why Dylan had traveled to Washington D.C.

"It's good to finally meet you. I'm Ace."

Dylan nodded, then rubbed his nape, not used to the feeling that was present whenever he was near a precognitive like Ace. It was nature's way of like recognizing like. He too was a precognitive like Ace and Zulu, and the other agents of the CIA program that had been compromised four years earlier and sent them all running for their lives.

"Zulu vouched for you," Dylan said. "He said you want to get the band back together." He kept his voice low while he scanned his surroundings, watching as the couple at the table closest to his was getting up to leave.

"That's right. He told me you were laying low in the West all these years."

"Funny. He never told me much about you."

"With good reason," Ace said quietly, before taking a bite from his pastry.

Dylan tipped his chin up. "What reason would that be?"

"I'm the leader of the band so to speak. If they get me, they get the others, and everything we know… Couldn't risk exposure."

"And what makes you the leader?"

Ace smirked. "I called dibs."

"Again, funny."

"Gotta keep your ability to laugh once in a while. The things we're dealing with are too serious."

Ace wasn't wrong. What they were dealing with was sobering. Dangerous even. And probably impossible to prevent. A nightmarish vision of death and destruction. The doomsday vision, Zulu had called it. It appeared that all the agents from the now-defunct Stargate program shared it.

"I know what you are. But Zulu mentioned that others switched sides. How can I trust you, and how can you trust me?" Dylan asked.

"The fact that you were hiding away in the West for the past four years already tells me all I need to know."

"And what is that?"

"You're still with us. You haven't switched sides."

"Why would I, after everything Sheppard gave me?" Dylan shook his head. Henry Sheppard, the leader of their program, and a precognitive himself, had given him a place to belong, a reason not to feel like a freak of nature. For the first time in his life, he'd felt that somebody understood him. But now that person was gone.

"I'm glad you feel that way." Ace leaned forward. "Now the question is: do you want in?"

Dylan looked at him for a long while. "Tell me something. When Sheppard recruited us, why didn't he put us all together so we'd know each other?"

"To protect us." Ace ran a hand through his hair. "Though I think he was wrong. We're stronger together, not apart."

"How many, apart from Zulu and you, are there?"

"On our side? Three others so far."

"You think that's enough?"

"No. But with everyone who joins us, we'll get stronger."

"To stop what's coming."

Ace nodded. "You see it too."

"Yes, more often than I care to admit."

Because the visions he had about a catastrophic event that he needed to stop were becoming more frequent. As if the event would happen soon. Maybe working together with men who were like him, precognitives with visions of future events, they could succeed and prevent this vision from becoming reality. But was it worth the risk of trusting somebody he didn't know? Could he put his life in this man's hands?

"It'll happen soon," Ace said, looking straight at him. "We don't have much time left. Are you in or out?"

"I don't know whether I can trust you. You know more about me than I know about you. Give me something. Something that tells me that *you* are still on the side of the good. That you want to get justice for Sheppard's death and stop the person behind all this."

Ace's jaw tightened visibly. "I'm his son."

Dylan sucked in a breath. He hadn't expected that. Zulu hadn't mentioned anything when they'd met in Washington State, other than a group of them was trying to find out who'd murdered Henry Sheppard, and take the bastard down.

"I had no idea he had a son," Dylan said.

"He adopted me when he found out that I was like him. I was a young boy, an orphan. I'll never turn against what my father stood for. And I'll never stop until I've found the person responsible for his death."

The conviction in Ace's voice made Dylan's chest tighten with compassion. He too had loved Sheppard and wanted justice for him. Maybe finally, nearly four years after his death, his killer would be brought to justice.

2

Zara Richards stepped on the escalator that took her out of the Metro station. When she reached the street level, the sun had already set, but the air was still warm. Her light summer dress was clinging to her, and she carried the blazer she'd worn in the morning over her arm. It was busy here too. The neighborhood was popular with residents as well as tourists because of the many great restaurants that lined the narrow streets.

She popped into the deli on the corner, picked up pre-packed sushi and a salad, before paying for her purchases and leaving the store. She wasn't in the mood to cook tonight, and she wasn't very hungry either. One of the other staffers in the office had brought pastries after lunch, and she'd indulged in the sweet treats.

With the plastic bag carrying her dinner, Zara crossed the street and walked along the next block. She glanced at the tables outside the coffee shop where she always bought her morning coffee on the way to work, when her heart suddenly skidded to a halt. She froze, unable to take another step or another breath, because what she saw jolted her to the core. She knew the man sitting at one of the outdoor tables in deep conversation with another. He hadn't changed much in the four years since she'd seen him last. Since he'd dumped her by text message. Like a coward.

Dylan Steele still looked as handsome as ever. His black hair was short, his skin a little more leathery than before. He had a five-o'clock shadow, which she'd always liked on him. He looked rugged, like a man who wasn't quite tamed, a man whose appearance had *bad boy* written all over him. Five years ago, she'd fallen head over heels for him. The chemistry between them had been explosive, and they'd been dating for nearly eleven months, practically living together, even though Dylan still had his own apartment on the other side of town.

She'd never understood why he'd left her from one day to the next. His text message still stunned her today.

We can't be together. Please forget me. I'm sorry.

When she'd tried to call him to find out what was going on, his number had already been disconnected. And his apartment to which she still had the key was still furnished, but all his personal items were gone. He'd vanished without a trace. Without an explanation.

The old anger churned back up inside her. She'd never truly gotten closure. She'd never had the chance to question him about his actions. They'd been so good together. Their relationship had been perfect, and fool that she was, she'd thought that they would get married eventually. Had Dylan panicked when they'd talked about renting a small house together? Had everything been happening too fast for him?

She'd never gotten answers to her many questions. But now she would. Because even though it was over between them, she needed to find out why he'd left her. Maybe then, when she heard the cold hard truth that he'd never really loved her, she would be able to finally kill the love she still felt for him. She would be able to go on with her life and not compare every man to Dylan. She would finally see his flaws and realize that she should be glad that he'd left her.

Zara pulled in a few steadying breaths and noticed that her heart was thundering in her chest, and her palms were sweaty. She could blame it on the humidity in the city, but she knew her physical state was a direct reaction to Dylan. The knowledge that in a few seconds she would be close enough to touch him, close enough to inhale his male scent, close enough to see her own reflection mirrored in his blue eyes, made her feel like a nervous teenager about to ask her school's quarterback to dance with her.

She shouldn't feel like this. She was an adult, and had turned thirty-six not even a month ago. She called on the anger that she'd tried to suppress for such a long time, and relied on it to lend her courage now. She'd always been somebody who'd avoided confrontations, but today, she wanted this confrontation. In fact, she needed it. She needed to tell him what a jerk he'd been, what a bastard to have dumped her so callously.

Lifting her chin, and pulling her shoulders back, Zara set one foot in front of the other, ready to tell Dylan what she thought of him.

ACE LEANED OVER THE TABLE, lowering his voice, while handing him a small piece of paper. "So we're agreed. Tomorrow at 9 a.m. This is the address."

Nodding, Dylan took the piece of paper and read it. "Okay."

"Memorize it, then burn it."

Ace rose and turned to leave. Dylan took another look at the paper, having already memorized the address, and held it over the candle on the table. It caught fire, and a moment later, he dropped it down on the table, where it burned completely, leaving only ash.

When Dylan looked up again, Ace was already on the

sidewalk, heading down the narrow road on foot. Dylan rose, leaving the half-empty plastic cup of iced coffee on the table, when he saw somebody come toward him. For a moment, he couldn't see the woman's face because of the headlights of a car silhouetting her. But a second later, the outside lights of the café illuminated her face.

He felt his heart stop, and he stood there as if suddenly paralyzed. His mouth went dry, and he couldn't form a coherent thought. He tried to recall what he'd been taught in his training as a CIA agent to deal with a situation like this, but nothing came to mind. He couldn't think straight. He'd never been able to think straight when it came to Zara, and that hadn't changed, even though he hadn't seen her in four years. Clearly, time didn't heal all wounds. Nor had it killed his love for her.

Zara hadn't changed a bit. She was still as beautiful as ever, maybe even more so now because he knew he didn't have a snowball's chance in hell of getting her back. He'd messed that up royally. He'd panicked four years ago, and by the time he'd thought things through and figured out a way to stay safe, and keep her safe too, it had been too late to take it all back.

"Zara."

She stopped right in front of him, her green eyes glaring at him, her long blond hair caressing her shoulders. She looked like a water nymph in the light summer dress in green and blue pastel colors. Like an apparition. Perhaps he was hallucinating, daydreaming like he often did when he thought of her. And of what he'd lost. Of what he'd given up. Of what he *had to* give up. Because he hadn't had a choice, not back then, not when he'd had to run for his life. Some nights, he dreamed of her, of the time they'd spent together, the plans they'd had.

"Dylan."

Her voice had an edge to it, one he'd never heard in her. It was proof that she wasn't an apparition, but real, because in a hallucination her voice would sound sweet and sensual, teasing and beguiling. Not pissed off.

"How, ahm..." He didn't know what to say to her. *How are you?* It seemed hardly appropriate.

Her jaw clenching Zara sucked in an audible breath. "You're back?"

The accusing tone in her voice wasn't a surprise to him. She had every right to accuse him.

"Yeah, I'm back."

"You owe me an explanation." Her voice grew louder.

Dylan glanced around, and noticed a single man at a table close by casting them a curious glance. This wasn't a good place for a conversation with Zara. A conversation that would get loud and ugly.

"I know."

"Then talk!"

"Not here." He reached for her arm, but she sidestepped him. He dropped his hand. "Sorry."

"I want to know why you left," she demanded. "After everything we had..."

He heard how her voice broke, and knew that if she cried, they would make an even bigger scene at the café, and with everybody taking videos of altercations these days, he knew his face would be plastered all over social media instantly, and his enemies would find him in a nanosecond.

"I promise I'll tell you everything you want to know. Just not here." He tried to think of a place where they wouldn't be overheard. "Somewhere private."

Zara nodded stiffly. "My apartment is two blocks from here."

He registered quickly that this meant that she'd moved since he'd left four years earlier. It didn't surprise him. For a moment, he hesitated, but he didn't have a better idea. The small hotel he was staying at was on the outskirts of Washington D.C.

"Okay."

As he followed Zara to the sidewalk and began to walk next to her in silence, he wondered how much he could tell her. She deserved the truth, but how much of the truth? Could he tell her of the precognitive skills that had made him and others of his kind the nation's most powerful asset? She would think he was crazy. And how could he explain to her why he'd had to go to ground four years ago, because somebody had killed the leader of the CIA's Stargate program, and was sending assassins after all agents? She would think he was paranoid. But paranoia had kept him alive. Several agents had already been murdered, and more would die, if Ace and his motley crew couldn't stop whoever had betrayed them.

Taking on their enemy would be dangerous. Could he really in all good conscience tell Zara about this? Did he have the right to scare her just to clear his own conscience by giving her the true reason why he'd left her and made it impossible for her to find him? She would be better off not knowing. Ignorance was bliss. But it would mean lying to her. And he was done lying to her. She deserved better. She deserved the truth, even if it didn't change anything about the past. Or the future, because they had none. Because after four years without him, Zara had moved on.

3

Zara crossed the street with Dylan walking next to her, silence spreading between them. Her heart raced. Too many things went through her head. When the other man had left the table, she'd watched Dylan burn a piece of paper, which she'd found strange to say the least. Neither of the two men had smoked, she was certain of that, so she certainly couldn't have mistaken it for cigarette smoke. And when she'd approached and gotten a look at the table, she'd seen the charred remains of the small piece of paper. Odd.

After his initial surprise, Dylan had quickly become calm and collected. It annoyed her even more, because she was anything but calm and collected. She was furious, and she wished she could yell at him right now, and pound her fists against his chest to make him understand how he'd hurt her. Instead, she'd agreed that they could talk in private, and idiot that she was, she'd invited him to her apartment.

How stupid! As if she wanted to be alone with him!

But she couldn't back down now. It would make her look weak. And she needed to look strong for this fight, even if she didn't feel strong. Just walking next to him, her old feelings for him bubbled to the surface. He'd always been able to make her knees weak just by looking at her. And even now, she had to stop herself from walking closer to him, because if she brushed up against him, her self-control would shatter.

Yeah, she had it bad. But she was determined not to let his charm steamroll her this time. All she wanted was to find out why he'd left her. And once she knew, she would be able to move on and live her life without thinking of him, without comparing every man to him, with none of them measuring up.

As soon as he'd answered her question to her satisfaction, she would show him the door. And that would be the end of it. And nothing would change that.

By the time they entered her third-floor walk-up, she was mentally prepared for anything. Dylan closed the door behind them, and walked into the small one bedroom apartment that cost half a month's salary. She noticed him glance around, but she was all out of patience.

Zara placed her take-out food on the coffee table, and tossed her handbag and her jacket onto an armchair.

"We're alone. Now talk!" She folded her arms across her chest, steeling herself for the truth. Had he left her for another woman? She didn't know what would be worse, Dylan having gotten cold feet because they were planning to move in together, or him falling in love with another woman.

Dylan cleared his throat. "I told you back then that I worked for a lobbying firm. That was a lie." He looked at her as if he wanted to check her reaction first.

"Why would you lie about your job?"

"Because I had to. I was recruited by the CIA over twelve years ago."

The news stunned her. "You're a CIA agent?" She shook her head, only half believing his claim. Anybody could say they were a CIA agent. After all, it wasn't something she could verify independently.

"I was."

"Let's say I believe that you were working for the CIA, that still doesn't explain why you left without an explanation." She brushed her hair back from her face. "Besides, if you were recruited twelve years ago, it means you were an agent when we were together, so don't tell me you left me because of your job."

Dylan reached out to touch her arm, making her realize that she'd started gesticulating like she always did when she was agitated.

"Please, Zara, hear me out," Dylan said in a soft tone, while he squeezed her arm gently to emphasize his demand.

He'd always been able to do this, to soothe her when she was upset, and now he was using the same skill to pacify her, but she couldn't allow it. She pulled her arm back so he had to release his hold.

"Then explain to me what happened. And don't tell me a CIA agent isn't allowed to have a girlfriend or a family."

"You're right. A CIA agent can have a family, many do, and I never thought it would be a problem. I worked out of Langley, not in some far away country. That's why I was able to be with you. To live a normal life." He sighed, hesitating. "But four years ago, the program I was in was compromised. Our leader was murdered, and the rest of us, we were in danger too..."

She furrowed her forehead. Dylan's statement sounded farfetched. But was it true? "What kind of danger?"

He dropped his eyes a little, his expression somber. "Somebody wants to wipe us out. Every single agent in the program. We had to go to ground from one moment to the next. When I got the word of what had happened, I barely had enough time to destroy all my personal records that might help my enemies find me." He lifted his eyes to look straight into hers. "And to send you a text before I had to destroy the SIM card on my cell."

She shook her head slowly. She didn't want to believe it.

"You could have told me where you went so I could see you, talk to you."

"No. At first, I didn't even know where I was going, and then, had I told you, my enemies could have found out from you where I was."

The assumption that she would have told his enemies about his whereabouts hurt. "I would have never told anybody! I loved you!" Tears started welling up in her eyes, but she forced them down.

"I know you would have never voluntarily given up my location. But these people have methods that can make anybody talk."

"Who are they?"

"I don't know."

"Excuse me?" She narrowed her eyes. Was he making this shit up as he went along? "You couldn't come up with a better story? Goddamn it, Dylan! I always thought you were a good man, but right now, I have serious doubts that what I saw in you back then was ever there."

Dylan reached for her arm again and took a step closer. "I'm still that man, Zara. But I had no choice. I had to run, or I'd be dead now."

She glared at him. "Just because you were a CIA agent? I don't buy it. There are plenty of CIA agents living normal lives here in D.C."

"That may be the case for others, but not for the men who were in the same program as I. It was top-secret. The things we know, the skills we have, they make us a target."

"What things? What skills? So your program was classified. What CIA program isn't? That still doesn't mean you had to cut and run."

"Damn it, Zara, why don't you want to believe me? I'm telling you the truth. I had to leave to survive."

She hit her fist against his chest. "You could have taken me with you!" The words were out before she could take them back.

"And put you in danger?" He shook his head. "Never."

"You want me to believe you? Then tell me why somebody wanted you and the other agents dead! Give me something! Something tangible. Not these vague explanations," Zara demanded.

For a long moment, he looked at her, and she could see the wheels in his head turning. "I'm sorry. I can't tell you."

"But you said yourself the program was compromised. And you're not in the CIA anymore. And suddenly you're back, four years later? Don't you see how that doesn't make any sense? Why stay away for four years, and then suddenly come back?"

"I came back for a couple of days two years ago."

"What?" Shock coursed through her. She felt betrayed once more. "And you didn't come to see me back then?"

"I did. But you were about to get married. I couldn't stay. You had a new life..." He shrugged. Then he took her hands and looked at them. "You're not wearing a wedding ring."

She remained silent, still dealing with the news that he'd been back two years ago.

"What happened?" Dylan asked.

She shrugged and withdrew her hands from his. Her fiancé, Tim, had never measured up to Dylan. Tim was a nice man, but their relationship had never been as passionate or as exciting as her relationship with Dylan. The closer the wedding date had come, the more she'd realized that she didn't love Tim, because her heart still belonged to Dylan.

"We broke up. I guess I'm not the marrying kind after all."

4

———

Hawk scoffed. He recognized a lie when he heard one, particularly when it came from a person he knew so well. But who was he to question Zara's words? Two years ago, unable to suppress his longing for Zara any longer, he'd traveled to D.C., only to find out that she would be getting married a month later. He hadn't even attempted to see her then, knowing that he couldn't stand in the way of her happiness. So he'd left again.

But it had hurt to know that she'd fallen in love with somebody else, and was ready for a lifelong commitment, while he'd never been able to move on. He'd had the occasional one-night stand, but he hadn't met any woman he wanted a relationship with. He'd always told himself that the reason was because he was still on the run, but the real reason was because he still loved Zara.

But he had no right to make a play for her again. Nothing good would come of it, and he would only put her in danger.

"For what it's worth, I'm sorry for having hurt you. And I wish I could go back and change it, but the truth is you're better off without me. Trouble follows me wherever I go." He sighed. "I have to leave."

He turned away from her.

"You're leaving? Fine! Go ahead: leave! 'Cause that's what you're good at. Leaving whenever things get too hard or too complicated."

Dylan whirled around. "Damn it, Zara! That's not who I am. And you know it. If I hadn't had to run for my life back then, I would have asked you to marry me and put a damn ring on your finger. When I found out that you were getting married to another guy, it broke my heart." He dropped his gaze so he didn't have to see her facial reaction. He hadn't wanted to say that, but now it was out. There was no taking it back. He might as well go all in now. "But it's too late now. I hurt you, and I understand that I can't fix what I destroyed between us. It doesn't matter that I still love you. I know when I've lost."

Without looking at her, he turned toward the door. He took one step, before Zara grabbed his arm, jerking him back forcefully.

"Damn it, Zara... don't... please... let me go..."

He could have easily shaken off her hand and opened the door, but he didn't. Feeling her hand on his arm brought long suppressed desires back to the surface.

Against his better judgment, he turned to face her. One look into her eyes, and he knew he didn't have the strength to resist any longer. Without breaking eye contact, he pulled her into his arms, sliding one arm around her waist, and placing a hand on her nape. A breath rushed out of her mouth.

"You should tell me to leave," he said without conviction.

"I can't," she whispered, and her raspy voice reminded him of how she'd always sounded when she was aroused.

"Baby," he murmured. "I'm still on the run. I can't offer you what you want—"

Zara put her hand on his cheek. "You *are* what I want." She slid one hand onto his butt and yanked him to her.

Instantly, his cock hardened, and he knew there was no going back now. "Fuck it!"

Dylan captured her mouth, and kissed her. Zara parted her lips and tilted her head to give him better access, and he took full advantage of it, delving into her mouth to explore her. She tasted of everything he'd missed about her: her passion, her tenderness, the openness with which she'd always greeted him. He'd been a fool to go without this for so long. Without Zara in his arms, in his bed. He would make up for it now and worry about the consequences later.

Zara kissed him with an abandon that told him without words that she too had missed him, and that her feelings hadn't changed. Everything about her was so familiar, yet equally new and exciting. Soft moans and sighs issued from her throat, and the sounds made him even harder. He'd always loved the way Zara responded to his kisses. And the way he responded to hers.

With every stroke of her tongue against his, his body heated, and more blood rushed to his cock, making him harder than a crowbar, and just about as randy as a sailor on shore leave. Needing to feel more of her, he found the zipper of her dress and pulled it down, so he could slide one hand underneath it. Something akin to an electrical charge went through him when his fingers connected with her skin. A visible shiver ran through Zara, and she grabbed his ass even firmer.

Encouraged by her reaction, he drew back just enough so he could push the straps of her dress over her shoulders and pull the dress down to her waist. Zara drew back, severing the kiss, and like she'd done so many times before, she snatched the seams of his shirt and pulled it up. He helped her and pulled it over his head, before tossing it on the floor. With his torso bare now, he drew her back into his arms. The moment her breasts connected with his chest, Dylan put his hand under her chin, making her look into his eyes.

"Zara..." He didn't know what he wanted to say. But he

wanted to capture this moment, because it was like the first time all over again. "I was a fool to leave you behind."

"Then make it up to me now."

Zara offered her lips again, and he took them and kissed her deeply, while he began to reacquaint himself with her body. Her breasts were just as firm as four years ago, her nipples just as responsive as they turned into hard little buds. He caressed them the way she liked it, teasing moans and sighs out of her body.

Zara wasn't idle either. She stroked over his back, before she slid her hands into his pants, gripping his ass firmly.

Fuck! If she continued like this, he would come in his pants like a green kid. He couldn't allow that. He needed to be inside her when that happened.

Dylan ripped his lips from hers, breathing hard. "Bedroom, now."

Zara motioned to a door behind him, while she opened the button of his pants and lowered the zipper. He had no choice but to rid himself of his shoes and pants here, if he didn't want to waddle like a penguin and trip over his own feet. When he was down to his boxer briefs, Zara had taken off her dress completely and now stood in front of him in only a tiny pair of pink panties. Sexy as hell, and innocent like a delicate flower.

He pulled her into his arms, and walked to the bedroom with her. She was still as light as she'd always been, and weighed practically nothing. When he'd first met her five years earlier, his protector instinct had reared its head, and he'd never been able to shake it off. A woman so petite, so beautiful, and so loving had to be protected at all cost. He'd fallen harder than he'd ever thought was possible. Zara was highly intelligent and independent, witty and caring, and the more he'd gotten to know her, the more he'd wondered why he'd been so lucky to win her love.

Dylan placed her on the bed, and stood still for a moment, just looking at her. Her blonde hair was fanned out around her head like a halo, and her flawless skin glistened. Without a word, she pushed down her panties and revealed her pussy to him. His heart beating like a jackhammer now, he took off his boxer briefs and freed his rampant cock before it could tear the fabric.

Zara's eyes almost sparkled when she dropped her gaze to his erection. The admiration in her look didn't escape him. He'd always loved that about her: she was like an open book, never hiding her true emotions, never playing games with him.

Unable to wait any longer, Dylan joined her on the bed and rolled over her. Zara spread her thighs and wrapped them around his legs just below his butt, indicating that she too couldn't wait to make love. There would be no foreplay, no delay, because they both needed this.

Dylan adjusted himself, and thrust into her pussy. Wet heat greeted him, making his descent smooth. Despite her juices, she was tight and gripped him like a vise. He'd never felt anything as intense as being inside her now, imprisoned by her strong muscles. If he died now, he would die a happy man.

"Oh, Dylan," she murmured on a raspy breath.

He looked into her eyes and read everything she didn't express with words. He saw the love there, the love they'd shared before he'd left. How had he been able to stay away from her for so long? How had he gone without her love for so long? It bordered on a miracle.

"I love you, Zara. I've always loved you."

Dylan didn't give her a chance to reply. Instead, he took her lips and kissed her, while he began to thrust in and out of her drenched pussy, finding his rhythm by reminding himself of how Zara liked to be loved. She was pliable in his arms and had always been an active partner in their lovemaking, touching him, caressing him, and expressing her joy, while asking for what she needed. Her moans and sighs, and the way she moved, guided him, helping him find the right rhythm and tempo, the right angle and position so his pubic bone rubbed over her clit with every thrust.

Their lovemaking had always been passionate, but tonight, there was more to it. It wasn't just passion that he felt, but what she gave him by welcoming him like this, finally stilled the longing he'd had for her ever since the day he'd left. The way their bodies moved in perfect harmony filled his heart with joy and his cock with even more blood. And while he'd made love to Zara hundreds of times in the past, tonight felt utterly new and tantalizing. He didn't want it to stop, so he held on to his control, and urged himself to concentrate on her pleasure, not his own. He slowed his thrusts, then rolled on his back, taking Zara with him, so she straddled him.

Zara released his lips on a gasp. Her mouth looked red and her hair was tangled; perspiration covered her face, and her skin had a rosy sheen to it. She looked like a woman thoroughly loved.

"Ride me, baby," he demanded.

Impaled on his cock, Zara moved up and down on him, her perfectly proportioned breasts bouncing up and down with every move, while her long hair cascaded over her shoulders, and one lock caught on her hard nipple. She leaned over him, offering her breasts to him. He cupped them and squeezed them, before he sucked one nipple into his mouth and licked it, then did the same with the other nipple.

He massaged her firm flesh, and reveled in Zara's sounds of pleasure. Knowing what she needed now, he let go of one breast, and dipped his hand to the spot where their bodies were joined. Like he'd done so many times in the past, he found her clit and caressed it. Instantly, he felt Zara's movements change. Her tempo increased, and her rhythm changed, showing him how she wanted to be touched. He had no problem following her lead, even though it meant tightening the leash on himself, so he wouldn't climax before her. With every ounce of his willpower, he held onto his self-control, and painted tight circles around her clit, increasing the pressure and speed.

A gasp that burst over Zara's lips announced the arrival of her orgasm, and he let go of his control. When her pussy clenched around his cock in quick succession, he climaxed and shot his semen into her.

Zara collapsed on his chest, and he wrapped his arms around her, and brushed her hair back from her face to find her lips and kiss her.

She let out a deep breath, and he hummed contentedly.

"Oh, baby, I missed this. I missed you," he murmured.

She lifted her head. "You should have come back earlier."

"Forgive me?"

Her forehead creased. "I shouldn't. You hurt me."

Dylan brushed his knuckles over her cheek. "I know. And I'm prepared to do anything to win your forgiveness." Even if that made him sound pussy-whipped, because for Zara, he would grovel without hesitation.

She paused for a few seconds. "Don't leave."

5

———

Zara felt something warm cradling her body, and tried to sink deeper into the wonderful dream of waking up in Dylan's arms. It was a dream she often had, though this time it felt more real, more intense. She inhaled the scent that was pure man and wiggled against the warmth at her back. A breath of air brushed over her neck, and lips pressed soft kisses to it, while beard stubble tingled her skin.

"Good morning, Zara."

She gasped and opened her eyes, awake in an instant. This wasn't a dream. Dylan was really here, in her bed, naked, and judging by what she felt rubbing against her backside, ready for sex.

"Dylan!" She turned her head to look at him. "You're here."

"I promised you I wouldn't leave." He smiled, while he gripped her thigh and lifted it so he could slide into place. "I have to go meet somebody at nine, but I have just enough time left for this."

He slowly drove into her from behind, making her gasp at the welcome invasion. "Oh, Dylan..."

"I've got you, babe," he whispered into her ear as he began to move back and forth in a slow tempo. "Just relax."

He cupped one breast with his hand and kneaded it. Her nipples instantly turned into hard pebbles. Zara reached back, placing her hand on his hip to urge him to take her harder. They'd both always enjoyed making love in the morning, and she'd missed this, missed waking up with Dylan in her bed, and his big body cradling her.

"I missed you," he whispered, while he continued thrusting his hard-on into her without missing a beat. "The thought of you making love to another man nearly killed me every day."

Zara slid her hand to his ass to intensify his next thrust. "After I broke it off with Tim, I didn't... I couldn't..." She hadn't had sex in a long time, because she hadn't been attracted to anybody.

"Oh Zara, are you saying...?"

She cast a look over her shoulder, meeting his gaze. She didn't have to answer his question, because his eyes told her that he understood. He lifted his hand from her breast and brushed his knuckles over her cheek. The tenderness of his gesture surprised her. While Dylan had always been a considerate man, he'd rarely shown the kind of tenderness he was revealing now. But before she could say anything else, he began to plunge into her harder and faster.

His breathing became ragged, and perspiration built on his skin. She allowed herself to be swept away by the passion he shared with her, reveling in the knowledge that she could still arouse him to the point where he was close to losing his control. She knew it, because he now slid his hand down to her pussy and caressed her clit with rapid movements of his index finger, setting her body on fire. She moaned out her pleasure, loving the way he took her from behind, his thick cock stretching her to capacity, while rubbing her clit with expert precision.

They moved in sync now, and she didn't even know where

her body ended and his began. She felt every fiber of her body, and the connection they'd always had. She sensed how close he was to his orgasm, yet he continued to caress her without rushing her to the finish line. He'd always done that, always made sure she climaxed before him, and she'd always loved that about him.

"Fuck, babe," he let out on a breath. "I can't hold on any longer."

She placed her hand over his, guiding his finger on her clit to adjust his rhythm slightly, and let out a relieved sigh, when she suddenly felt the dawning of her orgasm. "Almost, baby," she whispered.

Two seconds later, she felt the waves of her orgasm race through her body and explode outward. She let go of Dylan's hand, and on his next thrust, Dylan moaned out loud. A moment later, she felt the hot spray of his semen fill her, making every subsequent thrust even smoother. A shudder ran through her body, and Dylan hugged her closer to him, panting heavily.

"Fuck!"

She smiled and let out a breath of relief. She hadn't felt so sated and relaxed in a long time. "Mmm." When she turned her head slightly, she caught sight of the clock on her bedside table.

"Crap!" She shot up to sit.

"What's wrong?"

She couldn't help but notice Dylan casting quick looks at the door, then at the window, as if he was expecting an intruder.

"I've gotta get ready for work." She sighed, contemplating calling in sick, but the mountain of work on her desk would only grow taller if she did.

"Do you still work for that law firm?" He pulled her to him again, nuzzling his face in the crook of her neck.

"No, I'm a staffer for a senator now. So, I've gotta go to work."

"Haven't the senators already left D.C. for the summer?"

"Not yet, there's still another week before their session is over." She grimaced. "I'd better take a shower."

"Mind if I shower with you?"

She turned her head and noticed his mischievous smirk. "Only if you behave." Because she remembered only too well what Dylan's favorite pastime in the shower was.

"I don't know what you're referring to," he said grinning.

She rolled her eyes and pushed back the duvet, before getting out of bed. When she cast a look over her shoulder, she caught Dylan running his eyes over her body, his lips slightly parted, and his eyes turning darker. Damn, that look did something to her. She felt butterflies in her stomach, and was tempted to call in sick after all.

"Well, we'd better take a shower," he said and rose. "I've got somewhere to be too."

She let her eyes roam over his muscular body. He had even less fat on his body than when they'd been dating. His cock was still semi-erect, and she found herself pulling her lower lip between her teeth, suppressing the urge to toss him backward so he would land on the bed again.

"Woman," he ground out when he reached her. "If you look at me like that, you're gonna make us both late." He gave her a gentle slap on her backside.

Sighing, she walked into the bathroom ahead of him. Moments later, they stood in the shower, and warm water was raining down on them. Like they'd done so many times before, they washed each other. Zara enjoyed his hands on her, and loved exploring his body in this way.

"You must be working out even more than back then," she remarked, brushing her hands over his abdominal muscles. The ridges that formed a six-pack felt hard, yet his hairless skin was as smooth as velvet.

"I have no choice." He took a dollop of hair shampoo and

massaged it into her hair. "I have to be prepared, should my enemies find me."

"What will you do if they do?"

"Defend myself." He shrugged, before he rinsed the foam out of her hair.

"How?" She turned around and looked at him.

He met her gaze. "By whatever means necessary."

Despite the warm water, she suddenly felt cold. There was a determination in his eyes and his voice that she'd never noticed in him before. Had living on the run turned him into a hard man? She wasn't sure, because it didn't fit with the tenderness she'd noticed him display the night before.

Zara decided not to comment on his remark. Instead, she stepped out of the shower and reached for a towel. As she dried off, she glanced at Dylan as he washed his hair and rinsed the foam. The water pearled off his body, and his muscles flexed with every movement. Dry now, she brushed her teeth, while she continued to watch Dylan in the mirror. When he turned around and stepped out of the shower, Zara reached for another fresh towel and handed it to him.

"Do you have a spare toothbrush?"

She pointed to the drawer beneath the sink. "In there."

"Thanks." He began to dry himself.

"Will I see you after I get back from work?" she asked. She hadn't wanted to ask this, because it made her sound needy in her own ears, but the words were out before she could take them back.

"Is it all right if I call you later?" He rubbed his hair dry. "I don't know how long my meeting will take."

"Yeah, sure."

Zara hung her used towel over a towel rack and turned toward the door. Dylan put his hand around her wrist to stop her. She looked over her shoulder.

"Zara, trust me, I won't disappear again."

She nodded slowly. "All right."

She left the bathroom and walked into her bedroom. She slipped into panties and a bra, picked out a skirt and a matching top, and looked in the mirror, just as Dylan stepped behind her. Their gazes met in the mirror.

"You look beautiful," he murmured.

She knew he found her beautiful. She didn't doubt that. What she wasn't so sure about was whether he would really stay this time, or whether she would find herself alone again, without a means to contact him.

"I will call you, I promise," Dylan added.

"You don't have my new cell number," she said, turning away, an idea forming in her mind. "Where's your cell?"

He reached for his pants that he'd brought in from the living room, and dug into one pocket.

She stretched her hand out. "I'll program it in; you'd better get dressed."

"Yes, ma'am." He handed her the phone.

Zara shook her head, chuckling. "What's your code?"

He smiled at her. "Same as back then."

Her heart made a somersault. He was still using her birthdate as the passcode to unlock his phone? She felt tears well up in her eyes, and for a moment, her hands trembled. Dylan put his hand on hers, clearly having noticed how emotional she reacted to such a mundane thing.

"I thought of you every day," he whispered.

"I thought of you too."

When he turned away to put on his clothes, she entered her cell phone number as quickly as she could before she opened another app, typed in what was necessary, then navigated back to her own number to make a call to her phone. Her cell rang from the living room where it was still in her handbag. She'd forgotten to switch it off before going to sleep, like she normally did. Zara disconnected the call.

"You've got my number now, and I have yours," she said and handed him back the phone just as he slipped into his shoes.

Dylan took the phone and shoved it back into his pocket, before glancing at the clock on the bedside table. "I've gotta run, baby. Can I drop you somewhere?"

She shook her head. "I still have to do my hair."

"You want me to wait for you?"

"It's sweet of you to ask, but you know that it takes awhile."

He pulled her into an embrace. "All right then." He kissed her, one hand on her nape, one around her waist. This kiss didn't feel like a goodbye. It rather felt like a prelude to something more. Like a promise that he would be back, and they would be a couple again. She responded to him with the same fervor as the night before, showing him that she wanted him back, that she wanted a fresh start.

A sound like a low rumble rolled off his lips, and he ripped his mouth from hers. "Damn, Zara, do you have any idea what you're doing to me?"

He took her hand and pressed it over his fly, where a hard ridge greeted her.

"Oh."

"Yeah, oh."

"How about I take care of that for you later?"

"You'd better." He pressed another quick kiss on her mouth, before he left her apartment.

6

———

Outside the iron gate of the large mansion in the outskirts of Washington D.C., Dylan stood for a moment, wondering whether Ace had given him a wrong address, or if he hadn't remembered it correctly. Considering what had happened right after Ace had left the coffee shop, it wouldn't be all that strange that his mind wasn't at its sharpest and felt like a scrambled egg. Seeing Zara again after so many years had done a number on him. It would have been smarter to spend the night at the hotel he'd stayed at upon his arrival in D.C., rather than in Zara's arms. However, he couldn't regret their encounter, nor could he leave her again, and that threw up all kinds of problems, none of which he had a solution for right now.

One thing at a time, he cautioned himself and reached for the doorbell next to the brass plaque with the engraving *Sober Living Rehabilitation Center – No soliciting*. But before he could press it, a buzzer sounded, and the gate unlocked. He pushed against it, and it opened. Before he entered, he glanced up and looked into the camera that was affixed on top of the brick wall surrounding the property. Somebody took their security very seriously.

Dylan walked up the short path to the front door of the impressive villa surrounded by mature trees and bushes. The door opened, and Ace appeared in the door frame.

He nodded. "You made it." Ace stepped aside. "Come in. The rest of the gang is eager to meet you."

Still keeping his guard up, Dylan entered and glanced around the large foyer with the sweeping staircase leading to the second floor. Despite its size, the house gave off a homey feel. He inhaled. Maybe it was the smell of coffee and something freshly baked that gave him this feeling of being in somebody's home, rather than a sterile office or medical facility.

"Nice place," he commented, while Ace ushered him across the hallway to a door that was ajar.

"Thanks." Ace held the door open wider.

Dylan looked inside, noticing the dark grey walls first, before he cast his gaze over the desks and computer monitors, where several people worked. He entered, and Ace followed him. When the door closed behind them, the three men turned their heads in his direction.

"Hey guys, this is Hawk," Ace introduced him, before he pointed to one after the other. "This is Fox, our computer genius."

He nodded at Fox, who did indeed look a little geeky.

"That's Tiger," Ace continued, and pointed to a tall black man, who'd jumped up from his chair. He looked lean, and his movements were graceful like those of a cat.

"And that's Yankee."

The last man Ace introduced was a man who looked like he could be at home on any catwalk or model photoshoot. He wasn't just handsome; he was stunningly good looking like a movie star or a supermodel.

"Hey, guys, nice to meet you all," Dylan said, and the three men greeted him in return.

Then Dylan turned back to Ace. "So, where do we start?"

"I figured we'd fill you in on what we know so far." Ace motioned to the others, and everybody walked to the oval table in the middle of the room, taking their seats.

Fox brought a laptop with him, and put it down on the table, tapped on a few keys, and a large monitor on the wall across from the table flickered briefly before showing a desktop. Dylan hadn't even noticed that a monitor was mounted on the wall. It had blended in perfectly with the grey paint.

Everybody sat down, and Dylan took a seat between Ace and Fox.

"Let's bring you up to speed," Ace started. "Fox, the photos of the MRI machine."

Fox typed something on his laptop, and the screen showed images of large medical equipment.

"Looks like a fucking big MRI machine," Dylan commented.

"That's because it's really something else." Ace turned his face to him. "We know that our enemy is trying to create a quantum computer, and the data he's feeding it comes from brain scans of agents who have precognitive skills like us. By feeding the quantum computer whatever is in our brains that causes our premonitions, he's creating a machine that will be able to predict the future with amazing accuracy."

"How amazing?" Dylan asked, his eyebrows rising.

"99 percent," Fox interjected.

Dylan blew out a breath. "Something tells me that's not good news."

"Nope," Ace said. "It would give our enemy unimaginable power."

"How is he doing this? I mean, get brain scans. I'm assuming nobody's volunteering..."

"You've got that right," Tiger answered, looking across the table at him. He pointed to the image on the monitor. "That machine scans the brain. But it's so powerful that once it's scanned everything there is, it leaves your brain like mush. Your brain doesn't survive it. They got the jump on me. I was already strapped into that machine, and I would have died—" He motioned to the other agents. "—had these guys not shown up in time to save me."

"Fuck," Dylan ground out.

"Yeah," Ace said. "Tiger was lucky. But Smith and Jones already have the data from several of our agents. River and Echo for certain. We've confirmed that they're both dead. We believe there may have been even more."

"Smith and Jones? Who are they?"

The image on the wall changed. Dylan looked at the picture of a man in his mid to late fifties.

"That's Smith, as he likes to call himself, though we now know that his real name is John Bancroft. He's the one who runs the operation, hires assassins, scientists, and strong men who do the dirty work. But we know that he's not the head of the operation."

Dylan nodded, taking in the information quickly, knowing he had lots to catch up on. "You're sure he's not the head of it?"

"Absolutely. He's not a precognitive like us," Yankee insisted. "I was close enough to him. I would have felt it."

"No tingling then," Dylan said to himself. "And why do you all think that our enemy is a precognitive?"

"He has to be," Ace said. "The kind of information he has can only have come from somebody who knew about the program, and who has the same skills we have. He knows things he couldn't otherwise have known. And he knows that the only people who can stop him from achieving his goals are us."

Dylan nodded. "Let's assume your assumptions are correct, then you're saying that he'll try to catch as many of us as he can in order to feed our brain scans to his machine, and those he can't capture, he'll kill so there's nobody to stop him. Is that about it?"

"That sums it up," Ace said with a nod.

"Do you know what he'll do with the quantum computer once it's done?"

Ace shrugged. "World domination?"

"Start a war?" Yankee threw out.

"End democracy as we know it?" Tiger suggested.

"Take your pick," Fox said with a one-shouldered shrug. "Whatever he wants to do with it, it will lead to a terrible tragedy."

Yankee nodded. "The doomsday visions. I'm assuming you get them too, Hawk?"

"I do. Only in my sleep though. Not during waking hours like my other visions. I always found it odd." Dylan shrugged. "But I never had anybody I could ask about it."

"Well," Tiger said, "now you do." He motioned to the others. "We all have visions of massive explosions, all taking place in the D.C. area, we think. And we only get these visions during sleep, like regular nightmares."

It confirmed what Dylan had been seeing too. And these nightmarish visions were becoming more frequent. "I don't see an explosion. I only hear the loud boom. Then dust raining down on me, smoke filling the corridor I'm running in, screams of others fleeing... Carnage everywhere. But I can't tell what building I'm in."

Ace pointed to Fox. "Fox has figured out that he's in Smith's house in Fort Washington when the explosions occur. I'm somewhere at a military airport, seeing Marines carry a coffin from or to a plane, when the explosion hits." He tipped his head in Tiger's and Yankee's direction. "They're both somewhere near the Capitol when it happens."

"I see the White House, when there's an explosion behind me," Yankee added.

"And I actually see the Capitol blow up," Tiger said.

"Hmm." Dylan rubbed his neck. "Does that sound like the plot of *Designated Survivor* to you guys?"

Ace looked at him. "It's a possibility. But that leaves too many things to chance. No, I think Jones is too smart to do something so dramatic."

"Hold on," Dylan said, suddenly remembering something Ace had said only moments earlier. "Fox, you're in Smith's house, I mean, John Bancroft's house? And you know where it is? Have you—"

"I'm way ahead of you," Fox interrupted. "We put him under surveillance when we identified him a few months ago. He works for the CIA, some managerial position. But so far, we haven't seen him meet with Jones. Most likely they only talk on the phone."

"I'm assuming you've got a trace on Bancroft's phone?"

Fox nodded. "We do. But he's using a burner to communicate with Jones, and we haven't been able to hook onto it yet." He gestured to the many computers in the room. "We're well equipped, but some things are even beyond my capabilities."

"Yeah, and Michelle's," Yankee added with a laugh.

Dylan listened up. "Who's that? I didn't know there were any female Stargate agents."

"You're right, there aren't any," Ace said with a grin at Fox. "But Michelle isn't an agent, she's Fox's girl, and a pretty smart ex-hacker. Not sure what we would do without her. You'll meet her later."

Dylan shot up from his chair and snapped his gaze to Fox. "Your girlfriend knows about this? What the fuck, man! She could be putting us all in danger! Zulu didn't say anything about civilians being involved in this. That changes everything."

"Hawk, sit your ass back down," Ace said with an authoritative tone in his voice. "All our girlfriends know what we're doing here. And they're helping us any which way they can." He pointed to Tiger. "Without Olivia, Tiger's girlfriend, we would have never figured out Smith's real identity. And if Michelle didn't have such stellar hacking skills, we wouldn't have made such good progress in identifying what Jones is planning. Or in financing this whole operation with money from people who deserve to be robbed."

Slowly, Dylan sat down again. "So, Olivia and Michelle, they're helping you?"

"Yeah," Ace said with a nod. "And Lilly, Yankee's girl, is a doctor. So she helps us with anything on the medical side."

"Which is good news," Yankee said, "since Ace's fiancée is about to give birth."

Ace suddenly grinned from one ear to the other. "Yeah, any day now."

Stunned, Dylan stared at all four men. They were on the run like he was, but they'd managed to carve out some sort of private life and happiness for themselves. Did this mean that there was a chance that he and Zara could have that too? Could they too be a couple again even though he still had to live in hiding? But how did Ace, Fox, Yankee, and Tiger manage this? How did they stay under the radar?

Dylan shook his head, more to himself than to the others. "How do you do that? How do you keep your women safe?"

"We keep a close eye on them," Tiger said with a grin.

Ace laughed. "Yeah, I notice that *close eye* every morning when you guys come down for breakfast."

Surprised, Dylan looked at Tiger. "You live here?"

"We all do," Tiger said, pointing to the others. "Together with our girlfriends."

"Yeah, even Michelle and I moved in a while ago," Fox said. "Before that we had a safe house in the city, but considering that we stepped up surveillance on Bancroft, and spend every waking moment here, we figured we might as well sleep here too."

"Sounds like a commune," Dylan said. "And the house? Whose is it?"

"Mine," Ace said. "It was my father's. I grew up here. And before you ask: no, the house isn't in my name. It's in a trust, so that nobody can figure out where I am, and—"

"—and that's also the reason why we're not yet married," a woman said from the door.

Dylan turned to look at her. The woman was beautiful with dark hair and a belly so round that he knew instantly who this was: Ace's pregnant fiancée. Neither he nor Yankee had joked: she did indeed look like she would pop out that baby any moment.

"Phoebe." Ace jumped up and rushed toward her. "Didn't I tell you to put your feet up?"

As Dylan watched how Ace put his arm around Phoebe, he smiled to himself. An ex-Stargate agent could indeed find love. There was hope for a future after all. But first, they needed to find the elusive Mr. Jones.

7

Zara entered the large open-plan office in the Dirkson Senate building she shared with three other staffers. Nicky and Ben were standing over the coffee pot, gossiping, while Clara was busy opening the mail and sorting it into different baskets.

"Morning!"

Nicky and Ben greeted her in the same way.

Clara looked up. "Overslept?"

"My alarm was on silent," Zara lied. "Is he in yet?"

She tilted her head in the direction of the senator's office. She was rarely ever late, but she knew that her new boss was strict when it came to working hours. The old senator who'd died rather unexpectedly only a month earlier had been very laissez-faire, maybe because he'd held office for five 6-year terms and didn't have anything to prove anymore. He'd been a delight to work for.

"Sunny boy's got a breakfast meeting. But he'll be back any minute," Clara replied. "You're lucky. You can pretend you've been slaving away for hours. I won't tell."

"You shouldn't call him that," Ben interjected. "It's disrespectful."

Clara huffed. "If he wants respect, he has to earn it first. And so far, he hasn't."

"Just because he wasn't elected but appointed doesn't mean he doesn't deserve our respect," Ben added. "Besides, he's not the first senator who was appointed to a seat rather than elected."

"I do miss his father," Zara said, trying to steer the conversation into safer waters. "He was a good man."

"That he was," Clara said. She sighed. "And I'm not saying that his son isn't a good man. I'm just against the whole idea that he basically inherited his father's Senate seat without having to stand for election."

"But he will stand for election," Nicky said as she poured a cup of coffee. "There's only seven months left in his father's term."

"Exactly," Ben said with emphasis. "The voters will get a say soon enough. It would have been terrible if the governor of Idaho had left the seat vacant. There are way too many important bills that his vote is needed for. The margins are thin enough."

Zara took off her jacket and hung it over the back of her chair, before she placed her handbag in one of the drawers of her desk. She liked Clara and Nicky, but she could take Ben only in small doses. He was the typical ambitious staffer who would do anything to climb up the ranks and make the right political connections that would help him later in his career. He wasn't beyond sucking up to anybody just to get ahead.

Zara herself only saw her job as a way to making a living and staying in Washington D.C. rather than move into the suburbs. The work wasn't difficult and consisted mainly of dealing with the senator's correspondence, and helping Clara schedule meetings for him. She also spent a fair amount of time fielding telephone calls from constituents and triage what issues had to be brought to the senator's attention.

Zara grabbed the stack of mail that Clara had already placed on her desk and started reading it, making decisions on how to respond. By the time she'd gone through half the stack, making notes as she went along, the door to the office opened, and the senator entered.

"Morning," he greeted everybody cheerfully, and received the same greetings back from his staff.

He was a handsome man in his early forties, his looks very similar to his father's: a strong chin, chocolate-brown eyes, a tall stature with an athletic build. His hair was dark brown and full, while his father's had been almost completely grey at the time of his death. Not a single grey hair could be found on the young senator's head, making Zara wonder if he dyed his hair to make himself look even more youthful and virile. His dark-blue suit with the lapel pin that identified him as a member of the U.S. Senate, didn't look like it was from the rack. His fancy cufflinks only confirmed that assumption.

"Clara," he said, walking up to Clara's desk. "Anything happen while I was out?"

"You had a couple of calls," she said, looking at a notepad. "Your meeting with the Speaker of the House has been moved to 11 a.m., and the Senate majority leader wants to talk to you about the pro tempore vote."

"Thanks, Clara. I don't think I have time for the Senate majority leader today. Can you figure out a time tomorrow or the day after?"

"It sounded urgent," Clara added.

"Everything is urgent," he said with a shake of his head. "He can wait a day or two."

The senator marched toward his office. Zara took an invoice from the pile of mail that had arrived and rose. "Senator?"

He turned. "Yes?"

"I received this bill for utilities," Zara said and approached him, turning the bill so he could see it. "It's rather high and addressed to your father, but I don't recognize the address. It's not for the apartment he kept in D.C. Or did he have any other properties in D.C. that I'm not aware of?"

"Let me see." He took the bill from her hand and looked it over. "Oh, that's not addressed to my father." He pointed to the address. "That's meant for me."

"Okay," Zara said and reached for it. "I'll go ahead and pay it."

He didn't hand her the bill. "Not necessary. It's actually something I have to pay for from my private funds, not the taxpayers'. I'll take care of it."

"All right." Zara nodded, then remembered something. "Oh, and will you need me to show you the way to the Speaker's office since you're still new? It took me months to find my way around the Capitol when I first started working here."

He smiled, and Zara could imagine that his charming smile would convince many voters to cast their vote for him. "That's so kind of you, Zara. But that won't be necessary. Even though it's barely been a month since I've taken over for my father, I spent lots of time in both the Senate building and the Capitol as a kid and young adult, visiting my father. He showed me every nook and cranny." He winked. "I bet I know even a few secret hideaways that you've never seen."

"You're probably right. I worked for your father for only a year. It feels like no time has passed at all since..." She stopped herself, not wanting to get sentimental.

He smiled back at her, before he pivoted and entered his office, closing the door behind him.

***

It was mid-afternoon when Nicky rushed into the office, returning from delivering papers to another Senate office, out of breath as if she'd been running.

"Turn on the TV," she demanded, and pointed to Ben, who stood at a filing cabinet nearest to the television mounted on the wall.

Alerted by Nicky's insistent voice, Zara looked up from her computer and stared at her. Ben switched on the TV, and Nicky pointed to the news program. "There!"

Zara read the scrolling banner prefaced with *Breaking News* on the bottom of the screen, her heart suddenly beating into her throat. *Vice president's son gravely injured.*

Ben turned up the volume, when the door to the senator's office opened, and both he and Clara emerged.

"We have confirmation now that David Grossman, the son of Vice President Miriam Grossman, has been gravely injured in a friendly fire incident in Afghanistan," the newscaster reported.

Everybody in the office gasped in shock.

"David Grossman, who's a sergeant in the U.S. Army, is in critical condition, and is being flown to Ramstein, Germany to be treated at the army hospital in Landstuhl. The vice president and the president received the news an hour ago. According to White House sources, arrangements are being made..."

"Turn it down, Ben," the senator ordered. While Ben followed his instructions and muted the TV, he continued, "Nicky, find out what the most appropriate gift is that we can send to the vice president to show her that we're hoping her son will get well soon."

"How?" Nicky asked.

"Google it, or ask Siri, I don't care, just get it done," he snapped.

Nicky returned to her desk and typed something on her computer.

"Clara, get the vice president's chief of staff on the line so I can convey my heartfelt wishes."

"Senator, don't you think that's a little much? I mean, you've met Vice President Grossman only once when she swore you in. I'm sure the Senate majority leader will speak on behalf of—"

"In moments like this," he cut her off, "we have to act. We can't wait until somebody else makes a decision for us. A leader has to lead."

Zara caught Clara's raised eyebrows, but decided not to get into the conversation. For a senator who hadn't been in office for even a month, and barely knew the president or vice president, it was a little forward to make such a move, when it was the Senate majority leader's place to show support for the vice president. Only somebody who wanted to stand out, cut in front of the Senate majority leader. It meant stepping on several people's toes.

"What can I do, Senator?" Ben asked, showing his usual eagerness to please his boss.

"Find out what happened in Afghanistan, and report back to me. We'll have to launch an investigation into this incident."

"Of course, sir, right away, sir!"

"Zara, contact the chairman of the Senate Committee on Armed Services, and set up a meeting with him to discuss launching an investigation."

Zara nodded, even though she knew that her boss wasn't a member of the committee, and it wasn't his job to launch an investigation. Clearly, he was as overeager to impress the right people as Ben. And just like Clara's protest had led nowhere, Zara's wouldn't either, so she didn't even bother making one. She had more important things to worry about than whether he was treading on other senators' toes who'd served much longer than the junior senator of Idaho.

"I'll get right on it," Zara said and walked to her desk and sat down.

Not a single person in her office had made any comment on how the vice president must be feeling, knowing that her son was badly injured and half a world away. All they'd been concerned with was how they had to act in this situation to look good in the eyes of Vice President Grossman and President Mansfield.

It was the part in politics that she'd started to resent. She'd been naïve when she'd decided to work for the U.S. Senate, thinking she'd be serving the people of the United States, when in reality, she served politicians and political operators who were only looking out for their own best interests. Maybe she wasn't cut out for this kind of job after all.

She took a deep breath. Perhaps she was simply a little impatient today, wanting to get this day over and done with, so she could see Dylan again. There were still so many things he hadn't explained, still so many things they needed to talk about, because if he wanted a second chance, and if she wanted the same, they had to be on the same page. No more secrets. No more lies. Nothing less than an open book would do.

8

─────

I t was afternoon, when Ace and the other ex-CIA agents had filled Dylan in on all the intelligence they'd been able to gather. Dylan was impressed.

"Guess it does pay to work together," he commented. "Fox, you mentioned earlier that you were able to steal a list of Stargate agents from Langley. Can I see it?"

Fox nodded. "Let me get it up on the big screen. Maybe you'll recognize somebody." While he tapped something on his keyboard, Dylan turned to Ace.

"I'm assuming you all went through the list before. Did any of you recognize anyone else?"

"Only a couple of the ones who're dead now," Ace replied, then motioned to Yankee. "And this joker here doesn't match his own photo."

"What does that mean?" Dylan asked.

Yankee grinned. "I wanted to stay in Washington D.C., so I underwent plastic surgery so nobody would recognize me."

Dylan shook his head. "And here I thought you were blessed with those handsome good looks from birth."

"I wasn't too bad looking before either."

Everybody chuckled, when Fox gestured to the large screen on the wall. "There's the list. Go through it as slowly as you want."

Fox rolled his chair away from the laptop, and Dylan sat down on the chair next to his and scooted closer so he could use the mouse. While the other three men stood around, also looking at the screen, Dylan scrolled through the records. The list was bare-bones. Only a photo, the real name as well as the person's code name, and any special skills were noted on the list. The list was organized alphabetically by code name, with Ace being the first on the list. Earlier, Ace had told him that he'd been Sheppard's first Stargate agent, and that their relationship had been a close one from the time when Sheppard had adopted Ace from an orphanage in Virginia.

Dylan scrolled through the list. When he got to the record for Echo, he read the red overlay: *dead*, it said.

"What happened to him?" he asked with a sideways look at Fox.

Yankee answered in Fox's stead, "He went bad, switched over to the other side. They used him. By the time I got to him, he was already dying. They'd put him in that machine, fried his brain, though I didn't know that at the time." Yankee's voice was clipped.

"You knew him personally?"

"Yeah."

Since Yankee didn't volunteer anything else, Dylan continued scrolling. Fox's record was next. He noticed that the photo was rather old, and that Fox's hair was different now, longer, and his facial muscles looked more defined, the edges sharper, more angular.

"You look a lot younger in that photo," Dylan commented. "Do you guys know when those photos were taken?"

"Hey, we've all aged," Fox said. "And I look way better now anyway."

Dylan chuckled.

"The photos in the file were from the time of recruitment," Ace explained. "The earlier you got recruited, the older the photo."

"I see." He continued scrolling through the list. "No wonder some of these guys look like they're barely out of college."

"When did you enter the program?" Tiger asked.

"About twelve years ago." He was about to add something else, when he stared at the image that had just appeared on the screen. "Well, hello," Dylan said under his breath and turned to Fox. "Why does this list include agents who left the program years before Sheppard was killed?"

Everybody's eyes were on him, and Ace stepped closer. "What do you mean?"

Dylan pointed to the screen that showed the photo of a young man with a military buzz cut staring stoically into the camera, his jaw tight, his eyes expressionless.

"That's Polo. He got recruited the same time as I did. But he washed out within six months."

"Are you sure?"

"Absolutely. I recognize that face. I met him only a few times, but he always gave me the creeps."

"Tell me everything you know about him." Ace pointed to Fox. "Take notes."

Dylan shrugged. "I don't know a lot about him. But I know that like all of us, he had to go through a psychological evaluation. His profile came back, indicating that he was unstable and a borderline personality. Basically, the guy was batshit crazy and a total narcissist."

"How do you know all this?" Ace asked. "Sheppard kept those things close to his vest."

"I happened to meet with Sheppard when he'd just read the report on Polo. He seemed shocked, and I guess he needed to tell somebody. He told me that as much as he wanted to keep Polo in the program because of his precognitive skills, he feared that the man was a danger to everybody. Particularly because his precognitive abilities were off the charts."

"Better than anybody else's in the program?" Ace asked.

Dylan nodded. "That's how I understood it."

"If Polo was tossed out of the program," Tiger interjected, "and it's true that he's a borderline personality, then he would have taken this rejection personally."

Ace nodded. "Yes. He would want to hurt the person who rejected him."

"Sheppard," Dylan said. "He probably doesn't like the agents who remained in the program very much either. He may have thought they didn't deserve it."

"Particularly not if his skills are superior to ours," Fox added.

"You've got a point," Ace said. "We've always suspected that our adversary is another precognitive, because only somebody with our gift would be able to constantly stay a step ahead of us. At a minimum, we'd assumed that one of the Stargate agents was helping our adversary, but if what you say about Polo's personality is true, then he wouldn't be somebody who took orders from somebody else. He would be the one to give the orders."

"We can't know that for sure," Yankee cautioned. "Though I do agree that we need to look into Polo."

"Trust me, Yankee," Dylan said. "If you'd ever met the guy in person, you'd also feel that he's exactly the type of guy who'd go all out on getting revenge for this perceived slight."

"It's the best lead we have," Fox added. "But he won't be easy to find."

"We have his name and photo," Tiger said, pointing to the screen.

Fox tapped something on his keyboard. "Do you know how many men named James Johnson live in the US?"

Tiger shrugged.

"26,850. That's a big number." Fox pointed to the screen. "And that photo is old. I doubt he kept that military haircut."

"Military haircut?" Dylan said, thinking of something. "Can you check how many men named James Johnson were in the military about twelve to fifteen years ago?"

"I can certainly run a search. Michelle can help me hack into the system."

"How about facial recognition?" Dylan asked. "Do you have a system for that? I mean, yes, his hair might be different now, and he would have aged, but certain things don't change, you know, the distance between his eyes, the shape and length of his nose, his ears... all that could be compared to other photos like a fingerprint, right?"

"Sure it can. Michelle and I can set up some searches, and let the system do the work for us, but I'm telling you right now that it will take days to get any results," Fox cautioned.

Ace nodded. "Let's set it up. Run his photo and name through the military databases, and set up facial recognition for all other sources. Keep in mind that he might not have kept his real name and lives under an assumed name now. Our best shot is his photo, even though it's twelve years old."

"Can't you use aging software to see what he might look like now?" Yankee interjected. "I mean, assuming he didn't have plastic surgery like me?"

"You mean he could be as pretty as you now?" Tiger asked chuckling.

Yankee grinned. "You jealous of my good looks?"

Tiger simply rolled his eyes.

Dylan watched the exchange, smiling to himself. The camaraderie between the four men was evident in the way they ribbed each other and worked together so seamlessly. He'd missed that in his years hiding out in the Pacific Northwest. It was good to be with people who had a common goal and common skills.

When Ace had invited him to join them, Dylan had wondered how long it would take him to fully trust the other Stargate agents. He'd assumed that it would take weeks until he would relax in their presence. He hadn't expected that fitting in with them would be so seamless, and trusting them came almost automatically. He hadn't had this feeling since Sheppard's death. For the first time in four years, he felt at home among strangers, as if he'd suddenly found out that he had four brothers. Because that's what they were: brothers from different parents, connected by their gift of foresight, and united by their common goal to get justice for their slain leader, so they could all live in peace. Soon. Very soon, he hoped.

9

___

"Mr. Jones?"

The male voice was accompanied by a crackling in the line.

"The package is on its way to you," he replied. "You know what to do?"

"Are you certain, sir?" The other man cleared his voice. "It can't be undone."

Anger churned up inside him. He hated it when people second-guessed his decisions. They didn't know the whole story, had no idea how important every single cog in the machine was to achieve the desired outcome. Only he did. That was the reason he was the boss. He gave the orders.

"I'm aware of that," he ground out. "If you're getting cold feet, I'll get somebody else to do your job. But then you can't expect any favors from me when you need them. I don't deal with people who can't stick to the plan."

"No, no, sir, of course, I'm going to take care of it. I just wanted to make sure that's still the plan." His words fairly tumbled from his mouth as he backpedaled to remain in his good graces. "It will be done just like you said."

"Good. I'm glad we understand each other. Make sure to stick to the timing. It's crucial. We can't afford any delays in the delivery."

"I promise, sir! The timing will present no problem. Everything is ready. All I need is your go-ahead."

He rolled his eyes. He despised people who groveled so openly. He could never respect anyone who had no self-respect and caved so easily. But he needed people like that. They did his grunt work and could be disposed of when they weren't needed anymore. He wasn't stupid enough to leave loose ends. Everything would be tied up neatly in the end, and nobody would be the wiser.

"You have my go-ahead. When it's done, destroy your SIM card and the phone, and dispose of them. There will be no further communication. Got that?"

"Yes, sir."

Without saying goodbye, he disconnected the call. Tomorrow, the wheels he'd set in motion would be turning swiftly, catapulting him in the direction of the goal he'd been working toward for the last few years. Finally, it was time. Everything was ready. Soon, he'd have all the power he needed to crush the people who'd done him wrong. They would be like ants under his shoes: insignificant, without power, and dead.

10

For the umpteenth time, Zara looked at the display of her cell phone, but there were no text messages and no missed calls from Dylan. Was he ghosting her?

She'd worked late, the news about the vice president's son having resulted in dealing with extra correspondence, calls, and meetings. But now she was done for the night, and she wanted to see Dylan. She was disappointed—and hurt, she could admit that to herself—that he hadn't called her yet. Had he left D.C. again without a word like back then?

Well, this time he wouldn't shake her off that easily. She'd prepared for this situation. Determined not to spend the entire evening waiting for him to call her, she swiped to one of her apps and opened it. She tapped on Dylan's name within the app, and within seconds, a map appeared with a dot indicating Dylan's location—or rather, the location of his cell phone. She zoomed out a little. The dot indicated that he was in the outskirts of Washington D.C. When she checked the map, she realized that the closest metro station was too far away from his location, and she had no intention of walking around an unfamiliar neighborhood in the dark. It was best to take the car.

Zara went back to her apartment, and got her car out of the underground garage, then entered Dylan's location into her GPS and drove off. It took awhile, until she managed to get out of the downtown area, but the farther north she drove, the less traffic she encountered. On and off, she consulted her cell phone to make sure that Dylan was still at the same location, when she finally reached her destination.

Zara stopped the car and turned off the engine. But she didn't get out yet. Instead, she looked around to assess the neighborhood. There were many large single-family homes along the tree-lined street. Many houses were surrounded by tall fences, making it hard to see what lay behind. A few cars were parked on the street, but she saw no pedestrians. Most likely the residents in this area took their cars to get everywhere, rather than walk.

Zara opened the car door and exited, then locked the car, before she walked up to the house that her app identified as Dylan's whereabouts. The large villa was surrounded by a tall brick wall, though she was able to see the house, because the gate was made of wrought iron, allowing her to peek inside. There was light behind several windows on the first and second floors, though she couldn't see anybody inside, because she was too far away to make out any details, and mature trees and bushes partially obstructed her view.

Zara looked closer at the gate, trying to find where the doorbell was, when she noticed the brass plaque affixed to the wall next to the gate. *Sober Living Rehabilitation Center*, it read, *No soliciting*. She had to do a double take, and then glanced down at her cell phone again, wondering if she was at the correct address. There was no doubt: this was where the *Find My* feature tracked Dylan to.

What was Dylan doing in what looked like a fancy rehab? Was he an alcoholic? Had he gotten into drugs during the past four years? When they'd been dating, she'd never noticed that he'd had any problems with addiction. He'd consumed alcohol sensibly, and she'd never seen him drunk or acting in a way that indicated he was high.

Something was fishy here. She knew it instinctively. What if everything he'd told her last night wasn't paranoia but true, and somebody was really after him? Dylan had said that he had an appointment. What if somebody had set a trap for him, and they'd dragged him here, to this rehab facility? Images depicting Dylan in a padded cell wearing a straitjacket popped into her mind. What if he needed her help? Could she really in all good conscience walk away as if nothing had happened?

Damn it! She shouldn't have scruples. After all, Dylan had hurt her four years ago, when he'd walked away without a word. She owed him nothing. Still, she'd never been somebody who could turn her back when a person she cared about needed her help.

She cursed under her breath. How would she go about rescuing Dylan? She couldn't simply ring the doorbell and demand to see him. No, if his enemies had really captured him, they wouldn't give in to her demands. And if she didn't leave quietly, they would most likely lock her up too, or worse, get rid of her. Despite the warm evening temperature, she shivered at the thought.

She needed a weapon. She let her eyes roam. Her car was parked only steps away. Had she left anything in the trunk that she could use as a weapon?

Quickly, she walked to her car and unlocked the trunk. Inside it was a bag with gym clothes and sneakers. In one of the side pockets was a first aid kit. She let her hands glide over the interior of the trunk, when she suddenly felt something cold and hard. She gripped it and yanked it from its holding place. It was a tire iron. Perfect. She was about to close the trunk when she realized that it would be better if she took off her high heels, just in case she had to run away in a hurry. She exchanged them for her gym sneakers, before she took the tire iron again, and closed the trunk.

Zara walked back to the gate, examining it, before she checked out the wall to the left and the right, looking for a spot where she could climb over it. She looked more closely at the brick wall, but there was no way she could scale it safely. That left the gate. It was made of ornamental wrought iron, and had plenty of spots where she could find a toehold and climb over it.

She slid the tire iron through the gate onto the property, then gripped the gate with both hands. For a moment, she hesitated. Was she doing something reckless? Probably. But something was driving her to do this. Dylan had come back in her life, and this time she was prepared to do anything she could to keep him. Did that make her a crazy girlfriend? So what if it did? All her life, she'd done the sensible thing. She'd gotten a sensible degree, a sensible job, a sensible apartment, a sensible car, and in Tim, even a sensible ex-fiancé. But none of that had worked out in her favor. She was alone. And now she had the chance to get back what she'd lost when Dylan had left four years earlier, and by God, she wouldn't squander that opportunity just because what she had to do was reckless. For once in her life, she needed to do something that wasn't sensible. And she could only hope that it wouldn't bite her in the ass.

With a deep breath, she slid one foot onto an ornamental element of the gate and pulled herself up, then stepped higher with the other foot, until half her body was above the gate's top. Readjusting her hands, she swung one leg over the top, then followed with the other, and climbed down to the ground. Proud of her achievement, she felt almost giddy. That hadn't been so bad after all. She bent down to pick up the tire iron, but was all of a sudden jerked back.

She lost her balance, and a high-pitched shriek burst from her throat. Strong hands gripped her tightly, while she fought against her attacker. She managed to kick one foot back, but the soft soles of her sneakers did no damage to the shin of her aggressor. Suddenly, a tall black man stepped in front of her, and she realized that her attacker hadn't come alone. Zara turned her head so she could see the other man. He was just as tall as the black man, but he was Caucasian and blond.

The blond man kept her in such a tight grip that she might as well have been locked in a vise.

The black man with the lean body that looked like he could break her into two pieces like a twig, narrowed his eyes. "Who sent you?" His voice was a deep growl.

"Nobody," she pressed out and tried to shake off her captor's grip. "Let go of me!"

"Fat chance," the man imprisoning her said with his head dipping closer to her ear.

If he was trying to intimidate her, he was doing a good job. She had no chance of bending down to pick up the tire iron, and even if she did, she would never be able to fend off two guys at once. All she could do now was to pretend she was lost.

"You can't just attack me! I'm a law-abiding citizen!" She put as much authority and outrage into her voice as she could, but even in her own ears she sounded weak and scared.

"Didn't know that breaking and entering is considered law-abiding," the blond man drawled, sounding like he was from the deep South.

"Last time I checked," the black man added, "that was still a crime. So don't play games with us. We know what you're doing here. You thought you could slip past our defenses?"

"I got lost. I didn't—"

The black man snatched her by the neck, squeezing her windpipe. "Don't lie to us. Smith and Jones sent you, didn't they?"

Zara tried to shake her head, fighting for air. She had no idea who they were talking about.

"Fine," the blond guy said. "Let's take her inside. We'll make her talk there."

Finally, the black man let go of her throat, and she coughed and gasped, sucking much-needed air into her lungs. Her captor loosened his grip on her while he jerked her toward the house. She stumbled and almost tripped over her own feet, but the two men dragged her to the front entrance of the villa, her feet barely touching the ground.

Fuck! What had she gotten herself into here? She hadn't expected this to turn bad so quickly. She hadn't even had a chance to find out where they were keeping Dylan. Her chances of getting him out of here had just dropped to zero. And she didn't even want to guess what they would do to her now. They wanted to make her talk, which sounded like it would be painful. And her threshold for pain was extremely low.

The two men hauled her into the house, and she heard the heavy door fall shut behind her. The large foyer with the impressive mahogany staircase leading to the second floor was well-lit and sparsely furnished.

"Let go of me!" she cried out. "You have no right—"

"Drop your shtick! Nobody here is gonna buy it!" the black man snapped.

"They sent a woman?" a dark-haired man coming through a door from the right said, as he marched toward them. She instantly recognized him as the man Dylan had been talking to in the Café the prior evening.

"Nobody sent me!" Why didn't these men listen?

"Don't worry, I can break her," the blond man said with conviction.

"I didn't do anything wrong!" Tears welled up in her eyes. She was way in over her head. The first reckless thing she'd ever done in her life was turning into a catastrophe. And all she'd wanted was to help Dylan.

"Was anybody with her?" the dark-haired man asked.

"Not that we could see," the black guy replied. "But we should get ready in case we have to evacuate."

The dark-haired man turned back to the open door from where he'd emerged and called out, "Fox, get out here. We need to sweep the intruder for any bugs or transponders." Then he turned back and motioned to the black guy. "Check her handbag and strip her."

The black guy snatched her handbag and unceremoniously dumped its entire contents on the floor, while the blond guy pulled on her jacket and yanked it off her. When he reached out again, she slapped his hands away and twisted away from him so he couldn't touch her.

"No!" she yelled.

There was a loud sound coming from the stairs.

"Yankee, take your fucking hands off her!"

Zara whipped her head toward the familiar voice. Dylan was rushing down the stairs, wearing only a pair of shorts, his hair damp as if he'd just stepped out of a shower, a gun in his hand.

11

Dylan had been taking a shower in the room Ace had offered him to stay in, when the intruder alarm had gone off in the mansion. He'd quickly thrown on a pair of shorts, grabbed his gun, and stormed out of his room. At the top of the stairs, he'd heard Zara's voice, and a split second later, he'd seen her defending herself against Yankee.

He ran downstairs, his eyes instinctively roaming her body to scan for injuries. He found none, but that fact didn't slow down his racing heart. Several thoughts shot through his mind. How had she found him? What was she doing here? And had somebody followed her?

The other agents stared at him in surprise, and Yankee instantly took his hands off Zara, while Zara stared at him, mouth gaping open. Dylan shoved his gun into the back of his waistband and stopped in front of Zara.

"Zara! What are you doing here?"

Before she could answer, Tiger interrupted, "You know her?"

Without taking his eyes off Zara, who looked more than just a little confused and annoyed, he said, "She's my girlfriend."

Then he took her hands, and noticed they were trembling. "What's going on?"

"I didn't hear from you..." She swallowed hard, hesitating.

"She climbed over the gate," Yankee explained. "She was armed. We figured Smith sent an assassin."

"Assassin?" Zara gasped. "I'm not an—"

"She was definitely armed," Tiger added. "Looked like an iron rod." He narrowed his eyes at her. "And don't deny it."

"Maybe you wanna tell us what your girlfriend is doing here," Ace said in a calm voice. "You could have mentioned that you were expecting her to join you."

Dylan cast a sideways look at Ace. "I could have, had I known she would show up here." He looked straight at Zara. "'Cause I'm pretty sure I didn't give you this address."

Zara had the decency to look sheepish. "I turned on the *Find My* app this morning when I programmed my phone number into your cell."

Dylan sighed. "That's how little you trust me?" Maybe he deserved this. After all, he hadn't given her a reason to trust him.

"You didn't call."

"I'm sorry. The day got away from me. I was gonna call you..." That was the truth. He'd planned on going to see her after taking a shower.

"Yeah, well, you didn't." She glared at him. "I thought you'd been kidnapped, or run into a trap, or something, when I didn't hear from you." Her voice was getting louder. "After everything you told me last night, what was I supposed to think?"

"What *did* you tell her?" Yankee asked with raised eyebrows.

"Okay! How about you all butt out for a few minutes, so I can talk to Zara," Dylan demanded.

"Before you do that," Ace said, "you and I need to have a word in private." Ace motioned to a door on the other side of the foyer. "My office, now."

Since this was Ace's house, and he was running the show

here, Dylan had no choice but to respect his command. But before he followed Ace into his office, he glared at Tiger and Yankee. "If either of you lays another hand on her, you'll regret it."

Both men raised their arms in mock-surrender.

Satisfied with their compliance, he looked at Zara. "I'm gonna talk to Ace first, and then I'll explain everything. And don't worry: Yankee and Tiger won't hurt you."

Zara stared at him, looking shell-shocked.

Inside Ace's private office, Dylan remained standing. "What is it you wanted to talk to me about?"

Ace tipped his chin toward the foyer. "I need a little bit of clarification. You say she's your girlfriend. Yet she programmed her number into your phone this morning. That doesn't gel. If she were your girlfriend, you would already have her number in your phone. See how I'm having a problem with understanding this? Not to speak of the fact that you didn't even suspect that she switched on a tracker on your phone. Want to explain that to me? 'Cause from where I'm standing, it looks to me like you had a one-night stand that turned into a stalker."

"She's not a one-night stand. And not a stalker either," Dylan ground out. He paused for a second, trying to tamp down his anger at the implication. "Zara and I lived together four years ago. I wanted to propose to her. I'd already bought the ring. Then Sheppard was murdered, and I had to run. I broke it off with her via text message."

Ace rubbed his hand over his nape. "Fuck! No wonder she doesn't trust you not to disappear again. When did you go back to her?"

"I didn't. It was a coincidence. Zara saw us in the café last night. She approached me. We talked. I told her the bare minimum of what was necessary."

"About the Stargate program?"

He shook his head. "Only that I was in the CIA, and the

program was compromised, and our director killed, and that I had to disappear."

"And your premonitions? Does she know anything about that or what the program was about?"

"No."

"Hmm." Ace grimaced. "Do you trust her?"

"A hundred-percent."

"But she doesn't trust you, does she?"

He shrugged. "Evidently not, or she wouldn't have activated the tracker on my phone."

"At least that means she doesn't want you to disappear again. And considering she broke in here to try to free you, she still cares about you. But now that she knows this location, we have to make one-hundred-percent sure that she doesn't disclose this to anybody. Or she's putting us all in danger."

Dylan nodded. "I know."

"Do what you have to. Tell her you love her even if it's a lie. Keep close tabs on her."

"It won't be a problem." He wouldn't have to lie to her, because he still loved her. But he knew he had to tell her more about the situation they were all in, and the reason why he and his brethren were hunted.

"Good. We'll do more perimeter checks tonight just in case somebody tailed her."

"Fine."

Dylan turned to the door and opened it. In the foyer, Zara was still standing in the same spot as before, however she held her purse in her hand again, and the contents, which had been strewn over the floor earlier, had been collected. Yankee and Tiger waited with her, though they remained a few feet away from her.

Dylan met Zara's gaze as she watched him reemerge from the office and approach her. A million questions shone from her eyes, and he knew he needed to explain everything to her, or he would never regain her trust. He could only hope that she was willing to listen to the fantastical things that made him and the other Stargate agents special. And that she could set her disbelief aside when she heard the truth.

He was only a few yards away from her, when everything around him blurred. The loud boom of an explosion pierced his eardrums, and debris rained down on him. Stones and concrete broke all around him, while a cloud of dust blinded him for a moment. He heard screams all around him, but couldn't make out any words, because his ears were ringing. He wiped the dust from his eyes, desperately trying to see where he was, and what was happening. He turned on his own axis, but there was only dust and rubble. He let his eyes roam, searching for anything that identified the building he was in, when he spotted a plaque. *Speaker of the House*, it said. But before he could make sense of what he was seeing, he spotted a body amongst the rubble. He forced himself to step closer, and as the dust settled, his vision became clearer, and he recognized the person.

"Zara!" he screamed, knowing he was too late. Her body lay limp among the destruction. She was gone.

12

———

Zara stared at Dylan as he suddenly froze only a few feet away from her, his face turning into a mask of pain. She'd seen him like this before, many times in fact, and she knew what it was.

She approached, reaching for him. "Oh my God, Dylan."

But before she could put her hand on his arm to comfort him, Tiger jerked her back.

"Don't touch him!"

She whipped her head to look at him. "He needs help. He's got a migraine." They had been debilitating, though he'd always recovered quickly, even though he didn't take any medication for them.

"Migraine?" Ace asked, shaking his head. "Is that what he told you?"

Zara hesitated, finding Ace's question peculiar. "What else would it be?"

But Ace didn't answer her question, instead, he looked back at Dylan, whose knees suddenly buckled. Dylan didn't collapse, because Ace caught him as if he'd anticipated this. Dylan's head moved. He was breathing hard now, and his eyes scanned the area around him as if he was only just now realizing where he was.

"You're okay?" Ace asked.

Nodding, Dylan stared at Zara. Now on his own two feet again, he bridged the distance between them, and drew her into his arms, holding her so tightly she could barely breathe.

"You're here," he murmured into her hair.

"What did you see?" Ace asked.

Dylan released her, and she looked up at him, recognizing worry in his eyes.

"I was in the rubble of the Capitol. A bomb detonated." He swallowed hard.

"What?" Zara took a step back, shaking her head automatically. What was Dylan saying?

Dylan hesitated, and exchanged looks with the other three men. His expression serious, he finally addressed her, "I have premonitions."

She continued shaking her head. "No. You had a migraine attack."

"No. All those times when we were together, and you saw me like this, I had visions of future events. That's my gift." He motioned to the others. "And theirs. That's what the CIA program was about."

"That can't be. Are you saying you're a psychic?" She looked at the others, wondering if they would refute Dylan's claim. But all three of them looked somber. This wasn't a joke.

Before Dylan could answer, Ace interrupted, "He can tell you all about that later." Then he stared at Dylan. "Did you see who or what caused the explosion? Any details you can share? Anything?"

Again, Dylan swallowed hard. He reached for her hand, clasped it, then looked at her instead of Ace. "You died in the rubble of the Capitol. I saw you. I couldn't stop it. I was too late."

Barely audible gasps came from the three men. Zara's heart stopped, and she sucked in a breath and held it for several seconds, while her brain tried to understand the words that Dylan had spoken. She didn't feel her body anymore. She felt as if she was outside of it, looking at the scene playing out in the foyer of the large mansion. Maybe she was having a nightmare. Maybe she wasn't even here. What if she'd gone home after work, instead of following the tracker she'd activated on Dylan's cell phone? What if none of this was real? Maybe Dylan hadn't even come back to D.C. This could all be an elaborate dream she'd concocted to finally explain why he'd left her.

"Zara, did you hear what I said?"

His voice pulled her out of her thoughts. Her throat was too parched to form a word, her body trembling all of a sudden. She shook her head, and suddenly tasted something wet on her lips. It tasted salty, and she realized what it was: tears were streaming down her cheeks.

With his thumb, Dylan wiped away a tear and caressed her cheek. "I'm sorry, baby. I'm so sorry."

Finally, she found her voice again. "You have premonitions?" She glanced at the others. "All of you?"

All the men nodded.

"That's why somebody is hunting us," Dylan explained. "Because we see a catastrophic event in the future, and we may be able to prevent it. That's why somebody wants us out of the way."

"Are you sure it was the Capitol you saw?" Tiger asked.

Dylan nodded. "I saw the plaque outside the Speaker's office." He looked back at her. "Tell me why you would be in the Capitol."

"I told you yesterday that I work for the junior senator of Idaho," Zara said.

"Yes, but I thought you work in one of the Senate buildings, where the senators have their offices."

"Yes, but I have to go to the Capitol almost every day for one thing or another."

"Fuck!" Dylan cursed and rubbed his neck. He glanced at Ace. "I need to talk to Zara in private. Given my latest vision, I think it's paramount that she knows everything that's going on here so I can keep her safe."

Ace nodded. "I think you're right. Take her to your room."

Zara stared at Dylan. "You live here?"

"I do now," he said. "Come. Let's talk."

Still dazed and confused, she followed him as he led her up the large staircase to the second floor of the villa, where he ushered her into a bedroom at the end of the long hallway. When he closed the door behind her, they were finally alone, and silence wrapped around them. Zara gave the room a cursory look. It was warmly decorated, with a large bed, a dresser and nightstands, and an armchair with a reading lamp. There were no personal items in the room except for a small travel bag and some of Dylan's clothes.

Dylan reached into the back of his waistband and retrieved his gun. He laid it on the nightstand, before turning back to her.

Her tears had dried, but she wasn't ready yet to accept Dylan's words as the truth, though they did explain so many things. Why he'd left. Why he'd never taken medication for his migraines. But it didn't justify him leaving her without a word. Anger flared up in her once again, and she glared at him.

"You should have told me!" she railed, her hands balling into fists. "If you really loved me, you would have told me!" She beat her fists against his naked torso, while more tears welled up in her eyes. This time, she used her anger to force them down.

Dylan took hold of her fists and encased them in his palms, holding them pressed against his chest. "Zara, baby, I didn't tell you because knowing would have put you in danger. Besides, you wouldn't have believed me, and I didn't want to lose you. You would have left me if you thought I was a lunatic."

Zara sniffled, his words soothing her even though she didn't want to allow it. She wanted to remain mad at him, because she could handle *mad*, she couldn't handle *scared*. Because if Dylan really had premonitions, and what he saw was true, then she would die, and that scared her more than anything.

"Please tell me it's all a joke, or a nightmare, or anything, just tell me it's not true," she begged.

"I'm sorry, baby, but I won't lie to you ever again. I know the truth is scary, but this time I will be with you all the way. I'll never leave you unprotected again. I promise you that."

"How can you promise that? Didn't you just say it yourself? In your vision, I die in an explosion at the Capitol."

He released her hands and cupped her face. "We'll prevent the explosion from ever happening. I'm not gonna let it happen, Zara. I won't."

"You're one man, Dylan! How will you prevent this?"

"I'm not alone. The others, Ace, Fox, Yankee, and Tiger, they've already got leads on who's behind this. We've all seen parts of this event happening in our visions. If we work together, we can stop who's behind this. We have to."

His voice was determined, his tone beseeching as if he was trying to convince not only her but also himself. She saw it then, the fear in his eyes, the fear that he couldn't stop this premonition from becoming reality. Her resistance crumbled at the pain he tried to hide in his eyes. He was the man from four years ago again. The man she'd loved and trusted. She still loved him, but could they repair the broken trust?

"Help me trust you again," she said. "Tell me the truth. All of it. Don't leave out the bad stuff. I need to know the whole truth."

He nodded and sat down on the bed, gesturing her to join him. She sat down, leaned back against the headboard and crossed her legs. Dylan shifted, until he sat opposite her, looking straight at her.

"I always thought I was a freak because I had these premonitions, and the things I saw became real, sometimes almost immediately, sometimes months later. I had no idea that there were other men like me, until Henry Sheppard recruited me for Stargate, his top-secret CIA program."

Zara listened with rapt fascination.

"I finally felt that I belonged somewhere. Until Sheppard was killed, and the Stargate agents had to run for their lives."

13

Dylan didn't keep anything to himself. He told Zara everything he knew, even the things he'd only found out hours earlier. He explained the theory they had about the MRI machine being used to scan a precognitive agent's brain to harness the data to build a quantum computer. The more things he shared with her, he imagined the more fantastical the stories sounded, yet Zara listened patiently, and asked intelligent questions, which showed him that she understood what was at stake.

"So you and the others think that whoever is trying to build this quantum computer is going to be a danger to our democracy?"

"Not just ours," Dylan said. "If he can manipulate events, because he can predict them with the help of the data he's collected so far, he doesn't have to confine his actions to the U.S. alone. He can manipulate anything, any economy, any government, any country, anyone."

And if it was indeed Polo, the former Stargate agent, then there were no limits as to what he was capable of, given his psychological profile.

"He would be the most powerful man in the world," Zara responded, nodding. "He has to be stopped."

"We think that whatever he's planning will happen very soon."

"How do you know?"

"Several reasons: the frequency of our doomsday visions has increased, which leads us to believe that the event is approaching fast."

"Didn't you say earlier that you and the others only get this doomsday vision in your sleep?"

"Yes, why?"

"Because you were awake, and you had a vision."

"That's right. But we all have other visions of events happening, often involving those we're close to. Like you and me. What I saw today, the explosion in the Capitol, and you among the rubble..." He shook his head and moved closer to her until he could touch her cheek. "From the clothes you wore, I could tell it was summer. You looked just like today." He leaned in, pressing his forehead to hers, his heart beating with the fear that had gripped him during his premonition. "I can't let this happen. I saw you die in that vision so I would get a chance to save you. And I'll do everything in my power to prevent this tragedy."

Zara put her hand on his nape. "Could it be that what you saw today has nothing to do with that big event? Could it be unrelated?"

"Sure, but it's too much of a coincidence that several of us hear or see the Capitol blow up, while I have the vision of you dying in the rubble. I believe that the doomsday visions are rising from our sleeping hours into our waking ones. As if all events are about to collide."

Zara sucked in an audible breath. "I'm scared."

"I know. I'm scared too."

"You're scared?"

He nodded. "Even though I trained for things like this at the Farm. But I guess you're never really prepared for everything. And it's good to be scared."

"Why?"

"Because if you're scared, you stay alert, you don't get cocky, you don't underestimate your enemies. I'd rather have a bunch of people on my side who're scared of what's to come than people who are overconfident."

"You might be right about that." She smiled at him, and the action warmed his heart. "I'm on your side. And I'm scared. So I guess that makes us a good team."

He chuckled softly and pulled her into his arms. "A perfect team."

Zara combed her hand through his hair. "Yes."

"So, now that you know everything, are you gonna let me make love to you?" He shifted and pulled her onto his lap.

"But the others." She motioned to the door. "They're downstairs."

"So? This is my room. They're not gonna come in here to check up on us. Besides, all four of them have their girlfriends living here with them."

"All four? I only saw three guys."

"You'll meet Fox later. He's the resident IT genius. But enough about them. Back to my original question: will you let me make love to you?"

A soft smile curved Zara's lips upwards. "Well, since you're asking so politely..." She wiggled her butt on his lap. "...and are barely dressed, I think we shouldn't let this opportunity pass us by."

"I couldn't have said it any better."

Dylan sank his lips onto Zara's mouth and felt her yield to his touch. Her lips parted under light pressure, and she invited him to explore her. Still reeling from the tragedy he'd seen unfold in his vision, he kissed her with the passion of a man who'd stared death in the face. He didn't want to waste another second of their time together with talk about their uncertain future. Only the present counted right now. Because only the present was tangible. The past had already run through his fingers like fine sand, and the future was beyond his reach.

Tonight, he wasn't the ex-CIA agent who had all the answers, but the man who'd made mistakes and nearly lost the love of a good woman. He was lucky beyond all imagination. Lucky, because Zara was giving him a second chance. And nobody would take that away from him.

Zara felt soft in his arms, her curves cushioning his hard muscles, her sighs unlocking the door to his heart so she could make herself at home there, just like she'd lived in his heart before. He felt her hands on him, caressing his still damp skin, exploring him, teasing him in a way only she had ever been able to. His body awakened to serve its mistress, sending blood rushing into his cock, and catapulting his heartbeat into the stratosphere.

He felt his breath quickening, his hands now frantically pulling on her top to free her from it so he could touch the ripe fruit beneath. Impatiently, he yanked on her bra and managed to open its clasp. With a barely audible sound, it landed on the floor, while he was already opening the zipper of her skirt. It too landed somewhere on the floor.

When Zara opened the button of his shorts, he sighed a breath of relief. The zipper lowered almost by itself, and an instant later, he felt Zara's hand on his cock.

She gasped and released his lips in the process. "You're not wearing any underwear."

Breathing hard, he replied, "When the intruder alarm went off, I didn't have the time... Is that a problem?"

Zara laughed softly. "Not for me." She wrapped her hand around his cock.

"Fuck!" The sensation of being imprisoned in her soft palm was electrifying.

It took only a few more seconds, until he'd taken off his shorts and was naked. While he captured Zara's lips once more, he undressed her fully. Smooth, beautiful skin greeted him, and he let his hands roam over her body, relishing the sighs and moans she released when he squeezed her breasts and teased her nipples. She'd always been particularly sensitive to having her breasts caressed. He pressed her back gently until she was lying on the covers. He rolled over her, while she spread her legs wider, then wrapped them around his upper thighs to force him into her center.

He severed his lips from hers. "Somebody's impatient."

"You would be too," she said, pouting, "if you'd been through what I went through tonight."

"Did you really think I was in trouble?"

"Of course." She hit her fist against his chest. "I was scared that your enemies had caught you."

"Yet you came to save me. You're very brave." He brushed his lips over hers. "I think you deserve a thank you for your bravery."

"A thank you?"

He scooted down until his head was poised over her pussy. "Yes, a thank you." He inhaled her scent. "I didn't get a chance to do this last night."

"Oh, baby," she murmured.

ZARA MET Dylan's heated gaze, and her heart made a somersault. He was the same man again who she'd fallen in love with: tender, passionate, considerate. But there was more to him now. He was her protector now.

Dylan dipped his face to her center of pleasure and kissed her there, while he gently pushed her thighs farther apart to lay bare her most intimate place. A moment later, she felt his tongue swipe along her slit, making her flesh tingle pleasantly. She allowed a moan to roll over her lips, and pressed her head back into the pillow, enjoying his tender caresses. She'd always marveled at the skill and patience with which he pleasured her. There was no rush to his ministrations, no urging her to race toward an orgasm, but only a gentle licking.

Zara reached down to him to run her hands through his hair and felt him shudder. A moan bounced against her tender flesh, and a gasp stole her breath. She felt Dylan take her hands in his, and bring them to rest along her sides, where he intertwined his fingers with hers. He'd always done this when he'd gone down on her, and she recognized it as a gesture meant to emphasize their emotional connection. This wasn't simply fucking. This was making love, opening up to each other on a level that was so much more than the physical.

Zara concentrated on the sensations that raced through her body, entering every cell under Dylan's expert mouth and tongue. He increased his tempo now, and flicked his tongue harder and faster over her clit. Her breath quickened, and perspiration built on her skin. She couldn't hold back the sounds of pleasure that worked their way up her throat.

She didn't even care if the residents of the villa heard her. It didn't matter. She'd received terrible news only a short while earlier, the news that she might die, and all she wanted now was to live to the fullest with Dylan by her side. All anger about the things he'd kept from her, and the lies he'd told her, vanished. All that remained was her love for him, and the need to renew their connection.

Dylan suddenly released one of her hands, and brought it to her pussy. Now touching her with his fingers and his tongue, her arousal spiked, and she gasped and moaned at the pleasure he ignited in her. Every coherent thought left her, and she could only feel the vibrations of her clit and her approaching orgasm. With a breathless cry, she climaxed, her muscles contracting and releasing in quick succession, while Dylan stilled his movements and lifted his head from her pussy.

Their gazes met. His eyes were filled with passion, his lips still wet from their combined juices. Without breaking eye contact, Dylan scooted up so their heads were at the same height.

"I love you, Zara. There's only ever been you."

He pulled his hips back and thrust his erection into her to the hilt, making all air rush from her lungs at the forceful movement.

"Fuck!" he hissed. "This is even better than last night... or this morning."

Before she could agree with him, he took her lips and kissed her. She slung her arms around him, caressing his back, before sliding them down to his ass, and gripping him firmly to drive him deeper into her.

Dylan moaned into her mouth, her action clearly pleasing him. He increased his tempo and the intensity with which he took her. She'd always loved that about him, the wildness she could draw out of him, because it satisfied her craving for him, her thirst to be one with him. Her hunger for him grew with every thrust and every withdrawal. She spurred him on, encouraged him to plunge deeper and harder, to take her like he possessed her, like she was his. That knowledge filled her heart with warmth and her body with excitement.

Sounds of pleasure bounced off the walls of the room, and echoed in her ears. Every movement was smooth, their bodies glistened with perspiration, and their breaths comingled in a kiss that neither one wanted to sever. Time seemed to stand still, and only the two of them existed in this moment, a moment she never wanted to end. But there were laws of nature, of physics, that couldn't be broken, no matter how much she wanted this moment to last.

Dylan's cock was rock-hard and bigger than she'd ever felt him. She felt him change his angle by a small degree, and his thrusts instantly intensified, igniting her clit as if he'd lit a match to it. Her arousal catapulted her right to the edge of another climax. She hovered there for several seconds, while Dylan continued to slice in and out of her. He ripped his lips from hers, breathing raggedly now, deep moans tumbling over his lips, while the veins in his neck bulged as if the pressure was getting too much.

For a moment she feared that he was having another premonition, but then she suddenly felt his cock spasm and warmth flood her channel while he climaxed. Her own orgasm washed over her only a second later, and they both collapsed.

Zara was unable to move another limb. Dylan lay on top of her, partially supporting his weight with his elbows. She wrapped her arms tightly around him, not wanting him to leave.

"I love you, Dylan. I love you so much."

She looked into his eyes and saw her own image reflected in his deep blue pools.

When he shifted, she gripped his ass. "Don't!" She didn't want him to slide out of her. She needed this connection, because it made her feel cherished and safe.

"I'm heavy," he protested, though there was no conviction behind his words.

"I don't care." She'd always loved to feel his weight on her, and tonight was no exception. "I love feeling you inside me."

He chuckled softly. It made him look much younger than he was. There was a sparkle in his eyes, something she'd missed all these years they'd been apart. With his index finger, he tapped on the tip of her nose.

"You keep imprisoning me like that," he murmured, his

voice raspy and full of emotion, "and we'll never get out of this room."

"Do you *want* to leave this room?" she challenged.

"No. But eventually we may have to." He shifted his hips, driving his cock a little deeper into her again. He smiled and brushed his thumb over her lips. "This felt so good. Even better than I remember it. And trust me, I remember sleeping with you as being amazing."

Zara cupped his cheek, and he turned his head to press a kiss into her palm. "We always fit together perfectly. That hasn't changed, has it?"

He moved his head from side to side. "That will never change."

"But you and I, we've changed," she said, meeting his gaze. There was a seriousness in his eyes now.

"Being on the run changed me. But I think I'm stronger now. Strong enough to take on my enemies." He motioned to the door. "With the help of some friends."

"Have you known them long?"

"I met Ace yesterday at the café for the first time, and the others this morning."

She furrowed her forehead. "But didn't you say you were all in the same program at the CIA?"

"Yes, but we never worked together. Our director, Henry Sheppard, believed it was safer for all of us to not know each other. He felt that it may be dangerous for men with our skills to combine our powers and be tempted to use it for evil."

"Do you believe that?"

"Not anymore. I think we're stronger together. We'll be able to combine our individual strengths and our premonitions to find a way to bring our enemies down and prevent a catastrophe from happening."

"A bombing in D.C.?"

He shrugged. "That's not all, I think. Yes, there'll be a

bombing, possibly more than one, but we don't know yet to what end. We're not sure who or what he wants to destroy."

She remembered the code name he'd used when he told her about the suspect. "Polo? The ex-Stargate agent?"

"He's our best lead."

Suddenly a crackling sound coming from somewhere in the ceiling jolted her. Panic sliced through her, and she involuntarily shifted. Dylan's cock slipped from her sheath.

"Anybody who wants dinner, come down to the kitchen," the voice of a woman came through a hidden loudspeaker. *"I'm not gonna reheat for anybody."*

Zara let out a sigh of relief. "That startled me."

"I didn't realize either that they have a speaker system in the house," Dylan admitted and rose.

She ran her eyes over his nude form, admiring his toned muscles, and his graceful walk as he headed for the ensuite bathroom.

He looked over his shoulder. "You coming? You heard Lilly: she won't reheat dinner for anybody, and according to Yankee, she means it." He winked at her. "And it's time for you to meet the rest of the gang, since we're going to be living here until all this is over."

"We? Here?" Zara jumped up and walked toward him. "But I have an apartment in the city. It's easy for me to commute to work from there. I can't just—"

He put a finger over her lips. "You'll have to. What I saw is imminent. There's no way I'm letting you out of my sight. And there's no better protection than here at the mansion. From now on you have five well-trained bodyguards."

"But I have to go to work," she protested. "The Senate is still in session for a few more days."

"We'll talk about that later."

His voice was firm, and she knew what this meant. He wouldn't budge. "You're still as stubborn as ever."

He shrugged. "Yeah, well, get used to it. When it comes to your wellbeing, I'll never give in. I've lost you once. There isn't a chance in hell that I risk losing you a second time."

She sighed and grimaced. "Men!"

Unexpectedly, he pulled her against his naked body, his chest crushing her breasts. "You'd do the same if I were in danger. Hell, you broke in here to save me, not even knowing what kind of danger you might have walked into." He gave her a gentle slap on her backside. "And for that I should paddle your sweet ass. You're lucky it's dinner time."

He kissed her, and drowned out her protest.

14

Zara took a seat around the large dining table in the kitchen of the mansion. Dylan had introduced her to the other four couples, and she was worried that it would take her forever to learn everybody's name, particularly because the women called their boyfriends by their given names, whereas the guys addressed each other by their CIA code names.

"How did you all choose your code names?" Zara asked, looking first at Dylan, then at the other men.

"We didn't choose them," Dylan said. "The man who recruited us all into the Stargate program gave us our names."

"Oh, so, uhm, about the program. What were you supposed to do? I mean, with your premonitions?"

Dylan motioned to Ace.

Ace nodded and answered, "Have you ever heard of remote viewing?"

She nodded. "I saw something in a documentary once that mentioned it, but wasn't that program a failure?"

"It was. But only because the people the CIA recruited for it didn't have precognitive skills. Henry Sheppard, my adoptive father, was part of that failed program back then. However, he realized that if he could start up the program again, and find men like him, men who were precognitives, the program would be a success."

"So he looked for all of you. But how? I mean how would you even know that somebody is a precognitive? Anybody could pretend to have a premonition, no offense," she added quickly.

The others chuckled, and Zara took a bite of her food. "Oh, this is delicious by the way."

"Thanks," Lilly said. "It's your turn to cook tomorrow night."

"Oh!" Startled, Zara almost spit out her food.

Dylan laughed.

Lilly turned to Dylan. "Don't laugh yet. The guys here don't get off scot-free. You're on clean-up duty."

Now it was Zara who chuckled. Dylan smirked. "Not a problem."

"So, to get back to your question," Ace now said. "There is one thing that makes us recognize each other."

She furrowed her forehead, and looked at all five men in turn, but there was nothing that made them stick out as different. "How?"

"We feel a prickling at our nape when we're near another precognitive," Dylan explained in Ace's stead.

"Wow. That's astonishing! I mean, do you all feel that right now?"

"Yep," Dylan said.

"You get used to it," Fox said. "After living together with these guys for a few months now, I barely register it."

"But it's still there? Or does it fade?" Zara asked.

"It doesn't fade," Fox answered.

She glanced back at Ace. "Dylan said that you asked him to live here now."

"That's right."

"Uhm, he said, uhm that I..."

Dylan put a hand on her forearm. "Let me." He turned to look at Ace. "I told Zara it would be okay if she stayed here."

"It is. As long as you teach her how to spot if she's followed. We can't have anybody being followed here," Ace said looking serious.

"I'll take care of that," Dylan said. "Besides, she won't be leaving the house much."

Zara already opened her mouth to protest, but didn't get a chance when Phoebe suddenly winced in pain.

"Ouch!"

"What's wrong, baby?" Ace instantly turned to her, taking her hand and leaning in closer. He suddenly wasn't the determined leader of this motley crew of ex-CIA agents anymore. He was a concerned boyfriend and father-to-be.

"He's pressing hard on one of my nerves. I think I have to get up," Phoebe said and braced herself on the table.

Ace helped her up and supported her weight. "How about I take you upstairs so you can rest?"

"I don't wanna interrupt your dinner," she said softly, while she put one hand in the small of her back, exhaling sharply.

"I'm done eating anyway."

"Liar."

He laughed and pressed a kiss to her cheek. "I got you in this condition. Now I'd better take care of you." He turned his head briefly. "Night, guys. See you in the morning."

As everybody wished them a good night, Zara's gaze lingered on Phoebe as Ace led her out into the hallway, supporting her weight as best he could.

She suddenly felt Dylan's hand squeezing her arm, and looked at him. He smiled at her, and she knew instinctively what he was thinking, because it was the same as she was thinking: an ex-CIA agent on the run could be with the woman he loved, and could even have a family. Ace and Phoebe would welcome a child into this world soon despite the situation they were in.

Everything was possible if they wanted it bad enough. Did she and Dylan want it bad enough? Did they want each other bad enough to take this risk? To be together even if it meant they had to make sacrifices? Wasn't that what love was all about? To make sacrifices for the ones you love? To live every day as if it were the last, yet hope life would never end?

15

———

Dylan walked down the large staircase of the mansion. He could already hear voices coming from the kitchen. Zara had awoken just as he'd gotten dressed.

The smell of coffee drifted to him, and he followed the aroma into the kitchen. Sun streamed in from several of the windows, making the room feel airy and light. Olivia, Tiger's girlfriend was at the stove, tossing eggs into a pan, while Ace poured himself a cup of coffee. Yankee and Lilly sat at the table, drinking coffee and eating toast.

"Morning," Dylan greeted them, and received the same greetings in response.

"Sleep well?" Ace asked.

"Well, yes," Dylan said, grinning. "But not enough." And that was entirely Zara's fault. Well, maybe a little bit his too. After all, it was hard to say no to her, particularly when they had to make up for four years apart.

He was in a good mood. And that hadn't happened in a long time.

"Grab some coffee," Ace said, stepping away from the counter, after filling his own mug. "If you want food, just help yourself. There's bacon in the fridge, and eggs, and whatever else you can find."

"Thanks, coffee will be just fine." He rarely ate breakfast, even though today he felt hungry, despite the large late dinner he'd had. He poured himself a cup and joined the others at the table.

Across from it, the TV was on, though the sound was on a low volume so it didn't interfere with the conversations.

"How's Phoebe this morning?" Dylan asked.

Ace took a sip from his coffee before replying, "She only fell asleep a couple of hours ago. The baby is getting too big."

"Sorry to hear that."

"I'll look in on her later," Lilly offered. "The baby has been in the right position for almost four weeks. It could come any day now."

Ace sighed. "Are you ready for the birth, Lilly? I know it's a big responsibility, but we can't bring her to a hospital. Maybe I should have thought of it earlier and hired a midwife. Fuck!" He rubbed his neck, clearly anxious.

Lilly put her hand on his forearm. "I know you worry about the birth, but trust me, I read everything there's to know about home births; and I watched every video out there. I know what to do."

Slowly, Ace nodded. "Sorry, I don't mean to freak you out."

"And aren't you a doctor, Lilly?" Dylan asked, furrowing his forehead.

She turned her head to him. "Yes, but I ended up in research. Besides my residency, I didn't really work with patients. But in the last few months, living here at the mansion, I've had to apply my skills a few times."

Turning away from the stove, Olivia came toward the table, carrying a plate with fried eggs. "Lilly helped Tiger after Smith caught him and put him into that damn brain-sucking machine."

"You tell 'em, babe," Tiger said from the door. "A brain-sucking machine it is." He grinned, then winked at her. "She's an author and has a way with words, you know," he joked.

The others laughed, and Dylan had to chuckle too. Everybody in their group of ex-CIA agents and their girlfriends had different skills and strengths, and everybody contributed in their own way as best they could.

"Fuck," Tiger suddenly hissed and pointed to the TV. "Turn up the volume."

Yankee reached for the remote and turned up the sound. A reporter spoke from somewhere outside the White House.

"Reports have been confirmed that David Grossman, Vice President Grossman's son, died unexpectedly in the army hospital in Landstuhl, Germany. He'd been injured in a friendly fire incident in Afghanistan a day earlier, and had been flown to Germany for treatment. The exact cause of death isn't known yet, but sources say that he might have had a blood clot. An autopsy will be performed. The VP's office has confirmed that the coffin carrying David Grossman will arrive at Joint Base Andrews tomorrow morning, where it will be greeted by the VP and the president."

"Joint Base Andrews? That's not right." Yankee asked, turning away from the TV and looking at the assembled.

Fox and Michelle entered the kitchen. "We just heard," Fox said. "It's all over the news and social media." Fox pointed to his tablet, and he and Michelle approached.

"Fallen soldiers are flown to Dover in Delaware. I was in the army, I know," Yankee continued. "They wouldn't fly him to Joint Base Andrews."

"Could it be because he's the VP's son?" Dylan asked. "Maybe they're making an exception. Andrews is closer too."

"That's it," Ace said, staring at them, while he pointed his finger to the TV, where the news program continued, showing stock footage from a military aircraft where several marines unloaded a coffin with an American flag draped over it. "That's what I saw. Six marines carrying a coffin."

"Your premonition?" Dylan asked.

Ace nodded. "In my premonition I see them carrying a coffin. I felt the explosion, and I felt the heat. They were walking straight into their doom." He closed his eyes as if to recall more details. Without opening his eyes, he continued, "That's where it starts."

"If you're right," Yankee said, "if there is an explosion when the coffin arrives, then the VP and the president will die."

"Yes." Ace opened his eyes.

"That would make the current Speaker of the House the next president," Dylan mused. "Who's the new Speaker?"

"Johnson," Fox said. "Fuck!"

"You think he's James Johnson? Polo?" Dylan asked. It would all make sense then.

"Nah," Michelle said. "I thought his first name is Philip."

Fox tapped on his tablet. "Actually, it's J. Philip Johnson."

"What's the J stand for?" Ace asked.

"Give me a sec." It went silent in the room, and only the tapping of Fox's fingers on the tablet could be heard. He finally looked up. "His full name is James Philip Johnson, but he uses his middle name, because his father's name is also James, and he doesn't like to be confused with him."

Dylan felt excitement rush through his veins, and by the looks of the others in the room, they felt the same excitement.

"Photo?" Ace asked.

"Let's go to the command room," Fox suggested.

Everybody followed him. Fox sat down at the first computer and tapped on the keyboard, while Dylan stared at the screen. It took a few more seconds, before Fox brought up a photo on the large monitor on the wall.

"That's the Speaker. He's forty-one, so that would track with Polo's age, whom we estimate to be in his late thirties to early forties. But here's where it gets tricky," Fox said, pointing to a second photo, which depicted Polo. "The Speaker of the House was injured about eleven or twelve years ago, some sort of chemical accident. He had to have facial reconstruction, which means it's pretty much impossible to figure out if he's Polo."

"That tracks timewise with when Sheppard tossed him out of the program," Dylan mused.

Ace nodded. "Yeah. How about the eyes?"

Fox shrugged. "Easy to change with colored contact lenses."

"Aren't there any photos of when the Speaker was younger?" Dylan asked.

"I'll run a search, but so far, I can't find any that might help. I'll keep looking."

"I'll help you," Michelle offered and sat down at the computer next to him.

Dylan turned to Ace. "You think that Polo orchestrated this? That's a lot of moving pieces. How could he have known that the VP's son would be shot in Afghanistan, and then die?"

"He could have had a premonition about the VP's son, either his own, or one the quantum computer generated. He has some of the data, and the computer isn't fully ready, but what if the brain scans he already has are enough for this?" Ace asked.

Yankee sidled up to them. "If he knew that the VP's son would be injured, he could have taken it from there. I mean, he could have gotten somebody to kill him in Germany. It's not that hard."

Lilly nodded. "He's right. Someone at the hospital could have introduced an air bubble into his drip, and he would have died of an embolism. Hard to trace."

Dylan nodded. It would indeed be simple with the right connections and access. "He's sent assassins after us, so how hard would it be for one of his people to infiltrate the hospital in Landstuhl and make sure the VP's son dies, so that he'll be flown back to the U.S.?"

"Not hard at all," Ace agreed.

"And if he's the Speaker, he probably knows what the VP and the president would do in such a case. The VP and the president's families are close," Yankee said. "It makes sense that President Mansfield would accompany Vice President Grossman to greet the coffin."

"And boom," Dylan added, "you wipe out two birds with one stone. And a psycho becomes president."

"A psycho who has it in for all of us," Tiger added.

"One who'll have the power of the United States behind him. Nobody will be safe from his wrath," Dylan surmised.

And that wasn't a prospect any of them relished.

"We have to stop him before he can kill the VP and the president," Ace said, his voice determined. "Let's get to work."

16

———

In the room she'd shared with Dylan, Zara showered and dressed, then reached for her cell phone and switched it on. She'd made it a habit to always switch it off when she slept, even though she knew that most other staffers on the Hill kept theirs on 24/7. She preferred to get a few hours of uninterrupted sleep rather than be constantly available to her employer. They didn't pay her enough to sacrifice her private life for her work.

The moment her cell phone connected to the nearest cell tower, it began to ping with text messages and voice messages. She checked the latest text message first.

Where are you? It was a message from her colleague Clara.

Zara looked at the clock. She wasn't late for work, in fact, if she left now, she could probably make it in to work at her usual time. So why was Clara texting her?

She scrolled up to read her previous messages. They were all from early this morning. When she read the first one, her heart stopped and she gasped.

VP's son died in Germany.

She had to read the message twice, before she could trust her eyes. Hadn't they said the day before that the vice president's son was in stable condition? As she scrolled through Clara's messages, she learned nothing new, only that everybody was expected in the office as early as possible to be on stand-by for whatever needed to be dealt with.

Zara quickly navigated to her voice messages. One was from Clara who left her essentially the same message as she'd sent by text. Even Nicky and Ben had tried to reach her, Nicky leaving a teary message of how tragic this was, and Ben already asking if she had any ideas of what their office could do for the vice president to express their deepest condolences. Clearly, Ben wanted to look good as always, showing the higher-ups how much he cared—about rising in the ranks, not about their grief.

Zara sent a quick text message to Clara, letting her know that she was on her way to the office.

She received an instant reply back. *Thanks.*

Zara shoved her cell phone back into her handbag, slung it over her shoulder, and snatched her jacket. She still wore her trainers, but she would put on the dress shoes she'd left in her car later.

In a hurry now, she went downstairs. Even though she could smell the coffee coming from the kitchen and heard somebody handling dishes and cutlery, she knew she didn't have time for it. The door to a large room opposite the kitchen stood open, and she heard Dylan's voice coming from there. She walked to it and entered.

"Dylan?" she called out.

All five men as well as Michelle were present, several of them hunched over computer keyboards, others with their heads in papers, talking to each other. On the oversized monitor on one wall, two photos were displayed: one of a young man she didn't know, the other of a man she recognized immediately.

"Why's there a picture of the Speaker of the House up?" she asked, just as Dylan turned to her.

"Hey, babe," he said, approaching. "The VP's son is dead."

"I know. I got several messages from my office." She pointed to the picture. "What's going on with Speaker Johnson?"

"We believe he's responsible for David Grossman's death."

"What?" She shook her head. "He died at an army hospital in Germany. And I know for certain that the Speaker is in town this week."

Ace approached. "We're not saying that he did the dirty work himself, but we're pretty sure he staged this."

Dylan added, "We believe he's a rogue agent." He pointed to the photo of the young man on the monitor. "This is Polo, an agent who washed out of the Stargate program twelve years ago. We believe Speaker Johnson is Polo. And we have reason to believe that he is planning to kill the president and vice president when the coffin arrives at Joint Base Andrews tomorrow, so he'll become president."

Frozen in shock, Zara could only stare at Dylan and Ace. "But that can't be. The Speaker is a good man. I might not always agree with his politics, but he's a decent man."

Dylan shook his head. "Polo has borderline personality disorder. He's a psychopath. Being dismissed by Henry Sheppard after less than six months in the program must have stung somebody like him. His ego would have been hit by such a humiliation. He wants revenge. And how better to get revenge on everybody in the program than by having the resources of the Presidency behind him?"

"He's a megalomaniac," Ace said.

Stunned by this revelation, Zara stared back at the two photos on the monitor. There wasn't a strong resemblance between the two men, though she knew about the plastic surgery the Speaker had had over a decade ago after an accident. It was possible that the two pictures were of the same man.

"Oh my God!"

She felt fear travel up her spine. She'd met the Speaker a few times herself in the course of her duties, and he'd always struck her as charming and friendly. But didn't they say that even serial killer Ted Bundy had been charming?

"Do you know what exactly he's planning?" she asked.

"We know that there'll be an explosion when the coffin arrives on U.S. soil." Dylan pointed to Ace. "Ace had a premonition about it many times."

Ace nodded. "Although I never saw the VP and the president in my vision. Only the coffin and the Marines carrying it."

"And the bomb? Do you know where it will be?" she asked.

Ace shook his head.

"But we can't waste time on that right now," Dylan said. "Our first priority is to stop the VP and the president from going to Joint Base Andrews. They'll take Marine One. It's the only logical assumption. They wouldn't drive."

Ace nodded. "We have to stop Marine One from taking off. Disable it somehow."

"You wanna disable five choppers?" Zara asked, incredulous. "You're not even gonna get close enough."

"Five?" Dylan asked.

"Yes," Zara replied, "for something like this, there'll be more than one chopper taking off. Once in the air, you won't know which carries the VP and the president—at least three if not four will be decoys. The VP and the president might even fly in separate helicopters. How are you gonna stop them?"

"We'll think of something," Dylan promised.

She didn't feel as confident as Dylan sounded. How could he and his fellow agents deal with such pressure? She glanced at the others in the room, and noticed how everybody worked frantically.

Zara sighed. "I've gotta go to work."

"Out of the question!" Dylan snapped.

She clenched her jaw. "I have to, Dylan. With this, with the VP's son dead, I have to be in the office. It'll be frantic all day.

I've already texted my colleague that I'll be in shortly. I'm needed there."

Dylan stared at her, clearly torn. "Don't you remember what I saw? You can't go to the Hill today."

"You said that it's the Capitol that'll blow up, and you don't know when, and the Dirkson Senate Building is far enough away from the Capitol. I'll be safe."

"You can't—"

Ace put a hand on Dylan's arm. "She has to go. We might need somebody on the Hill, in case there's chatter that we should know about."

Dylan glared at Ace. "You're suggesting we rope her in? No way! It's too dangerous."

Zara put her hand on Dylan's chest. "I promise I'll go nowhere near the Capitol. I'll stay in the Senate Building, and if anybody asks me to go to the Capitol, I'll figure out an excuse of why not to go. All right?"

For a long few seconds, Dylan said nothing, and she could see his mind working. Finally, he nodded.

"Fine, but I'll need the location tracker on." He reached out his hand.

She retrieved her cell phone from her handbag and unlocked it, before handing it to him. He tapped on it for a few moments, before handing it back to her.

Dylan looked straight into her eyes. "And if I see that you're getting anywhere near the Capitol, I'll be on your ass like white on rice. Do we understand each other?"

Zara grunted in displeasure. She hated that side of him. "Has anybody ever told you that you sound like a drill sergeant?"

"No. And you're not answering my question." He went toe to toe with her.

"Fine! I promise."

She sighed and pivoted, ready to head for the door, when Dylan pulled her back and drew her into his arms. His lips were on hers a second later, and his kiss felt as if he was branding her to show everybody that she was his. To her surprise, she yielded to his kiss. He released her as quickly as he'd grabbed her.

As she walked toward the door, Tiger called after her, "Oh, and Zara, your car is parked behind the house. I'll open the gate remotely for you when I see you on the security camera. Your car keys are on the table in the foyer."

She acknowledged his words with a quick nod and left.

17

———

It was noon when Olivia and Lilly brought food to the command center so they could eat while they were working. Fox had mirrored Dylan's cell phone apps with one of the computers so he could keep an eye on Zara's location on the monitor without having to constantly check his cell. Everybody was applying their skills to come up with a plan of how to prevent the president and the vice president from being killed.

"How would you smuggle a bomb into Joint Base Andrews?" Yankee mused.

"Security is really tight there. It has to be an inside job, right?" Dylan asked, looking at Ace, who chewed on a sandwich.

"We have to assume that Polo has contacts in the military. Maybe he's cashing in an old favor," Fox said from behind his computer, taking a quick break from hacking away on his keyboard.

"Still, even if he's got one person on the inside," Yankee said, "everything that goes into that place is screened. We're not talking about a firecracker, are we, Ace?"

Ace shook his head. "No. Definitely a big explosion. It's not something you could smuggle in on your body. It has to be big enough to blow the president and the VP to smithereens wherever they're standing."

Ace's words sparked a thought in Dylan. "They would be close to the coffin, right, I mean the VP and the president?"

Everybody nodded.

"What are you thinking?" Ace asked.

"What if they don't have to get the bomb past their security? What if it lands there?"

His fellow agents' eyes widened.

"You mean—" Tiger stopped himself from completing his sentence, nodding to himself.

Dylan nodded. "The coffin. They're not gonna open the coffin when it arrives at Andrews."

"Fuck!" Ace cursed.

"It's brilliant, really," Tiger agreed.

Yankee grunted to himself. "Security on the base in Germany is maybe a little less strict. And if the body is put into the coffin at the army hospital in Landstuhl, and not opened again, then whoever made sure that David Grossman didn't make it, also planted the bomb in his coffin."

"Sounds doable," Ace mused. "But how is he detonating the bomb?"

"Can't be a timer," Fox said instantly, standing up from his chair now. "Too many variables. If the plane gets delayed due to weather, or rerouted, then chances are that the bomb goes off when the plane is still in the air."

"You're right," Dylan agreed. "That leaves remote detonation. Doable right?"

Fox nodded. "Totally. But Polo would have to know the exact time the president and the VP are close enough to the coffin. And I'm not aware that the Speaker of the House is going to Andrews with them."

Dylan shook his head. "He can do what he needs to do from

any TV. The press is gonna cover this event live, right? He will see when it's the right moment."

"Fuck!" Ace ran a hand through his hair.

Lilly, who'd stood close to Yankee, suddenly cleared her throat. "Can't you call in a bomb scare or something? An anonymous tip?"

Dylan exchanged a look with Ace, and they both shook their heads.

"We have nothing that ties the Speaker to the bomb. And we can't spook him," Ace said with regret.

"We have to eliminate him first. If he finds out we're onto him, he might disappear," Dylan added. "We can't let on that we know of his plan. Everything we do has to look like it's an accident or a believable coincidence."

Yankee looked at Lilly. "Nice suggestion though."

Lilly shrugged. "Well, that was my two cents." She grabbed the serving tray. "Oh, Ace, you should look in on Phoebe. She complained of back pain. I can't give her anything for it, but maybe you can massage her back a little to help her with the pain? Or I can do it..."

Ace jumped up. "I'll do it. I need to clear my head anyway." He followed Lilly out of the room and closed the door behind him.

"Can't be easy for him right now with all that's going on," Dylan mused. "I hope she'll be all right." He'd seen Phoebe only during dinner the night before. She'd looked tired and had moved sluggishly.

"Phoebe is strong," Michelle commented.

"And Ace can handle a lot more than we think," Fox said, sitting back down in his chair. "But if push comes to shove, we can cover for him."

"Well, then we'd better come up with a brilliant idea of how to prevent this disaster," Dylan said, looking at the others. "So if we can't disable the bomb, we'll have to stop the president and the VP from getting onto Marine One."

"Yeah, but if we disable Marine One somehow," Tiger said skeptically, "then they'll take ground transportation. Takes longer, but they'll still get there."

"Not necessarily," Fox suddenly said.

Everybody turned to him, waiting for an explanation to his cryptic words.

"Meaning?" Dylan asked finally.

"I think I have an idea of how to disable all helicopters in the vicinity, and making sure that the Secret Service will take the president and VP to the bunker under the White House," Fox explained.

Several pairs of eyebrows rose.

"And how are we gonna do that? You know anybody in the Secret Service?" Yankee asked.

"No," Fox said, "but I know what their protocols are. If they believe there is a direct threat against POTUS and VPOTUS, they'll follow protocol."

"What about Polo? Won't he get suspicious?" Dylan asked.

Fox shrugged. "Secret Service won't immediately disclose why they're taking their charges to the bunker. If everything runs like I expect it, we're buying ourselves a few hours of time. If we're lucky, enough to snatch Polo."

"All right," Dylan said. "What do you need us to do?"

18

Things were moving along at the right pace. Polo looked out the window of his living room in his condo, where only a dim reading lamp provided some illumination. He could observe the goings-on outside without being seen. Not that it mattered right now. Nobody suspected him of any wrongdoing. He'd been careful, making sure that nobody could tie him to the events that would unfold tomorrow.

For the first time in a long time, he felt satisfied. Soon, he would have all he desired, and his enemies and everybody else who stood in the way of his plan, would meet with a swift, but bloody end. The power he'd soon have, was almost palpable now. And nobody would ever be casting him out as if he didn't measure up. The anger he felt about Henry Sheppard's betrayal still tasted bitter on his tongue, even now, many years later. Sheppard had been unjust in his treatment of him. He'd preferred his other agents to him, casting him out as if he was a leper, even though his precognitive skills were more pronounced and sharper than those of the other agents. Sheppard had said so himself shortly after Polo had started his training with the CIA.

Nevertheless, he'd expelled him from the program after less than six months, claiming he wasn't suited for the Stargate program.

Bullshit! Polo alone understood that a power like foresight shouldn't be squandered on a CIA program that had no real goal, but that of preventing disasters. He didn't give a flying fuck about preventing disasters. He knew that his gift could be harnessed to bring other governments to heel, showing them that the U.S. was all powerful and the only superpower left. A superpower with a leader who understood how to control other nations.

It had taken him longer than he'd expected to put everything in place to ensure that his plan would come off without a hitch. Unfortunately, he'd had to work with idiots like Smith, who'd failed multiple times at the tasks he'd been given. But soon, even that incompetent fool would be taken care of so he could never again throw a wrench into the plans Polo had so carefully orchestrated.

He turned away from the D.C. skyline and walked to the drinks cabinet, where he poured himself a twenty-year old scotch. He drank it down in one gulp, savoring the taste. Maybe a celebratory drink was a little early, but nobody could stop him now. Everything was set and would happen like clockwork, one domino would make the next fall and cause a chain reaction that was inevitable.

A cell phone rang, the sound piercing the silence in his condo. It was his burner, the phone he used exclusively to communicate with Smith. He had a separate burner to contact the few operatives who executed things he couldn't have Smith handle.

"Yes?"

"Mr. Jones, it's Smith."

He'd expected the call. "Mr. Smith. About time you called me back."

"I'm sorry," the whimpering fool groveled, "but I was somewhere where I couldn't talk in private."

"Hmm."

"You wanted to talk to me?"

"Yes," Polo began. "Listen carefully: everything is set. Tomorrow, don't leave your house if you don't want to become a casualty in the events I've set in motion."

"But, why—"

He hated to be interrupted. "I didn't say talk. I said listen." He grunted in displeasure.

"Apologies."

"Stay at home tomorrow, no matter what happens. Keep your regular cellphone and your burner switched on. It's important. Your cellphone may provide you with an alibi should any of the events tomorrow be linked to you. And should anything change, I need to be able to reach you on the burner. Do you understand?"

"Yes."

"Good. In the morning you will call your office and tell them you have food poisoning and will stay at home."

"All right."

"Good. It's paramount that you follow these instructions to a T. I can't have anything threatening my plans tomorrow."

"You can count on me... uhm..."

"Yes? What else?"

"Uhm... the money, you know, for my services... when can I expect the funds in my account?"

Polo scoffed silently. Smith wasn't any better than a common whore. He sold himself for money, whereas Polo believed in something.

"You'll receive what is due to you by the end of tomorrow." And that wasn't even a lie. Smith would indeed receive what he deserved.

"Thank you, sir, I appreciate it."

There was something akin to relief in Smith's tone of voice. If only the fool knew what he deserved, but weasels like Smith had no idea of their true value. Or lack thereof.

"Thank you for your service," Polo said and disconnected the call.

He turned the cellphone around, opened up the back of it, and took out the SIM card. He placed it in a marble ashtray, took a decorative paperweight from the coffee table and smashed the SIM card with it.

There would be no more communications with Smith.

19

———

"Are you sure you can get us in?" Dylan asked, giving Zara a sideways look as she maneuvered her car through early morning D.C. traffic. He sat in the passenger seat, while Tiger sat behind him.

"As long as you get through the metal detector at the Dirkson Senate building, you're good to get into the Capitol," she assured him. "I'll have visitor passes ready for both of you. Make sure you text me before you get there, so I can meet you in the lobby."

Dylan nodded. They'd discussed every detail of their plan several times to make sure everybody knew what they needed to do.

"And don't bring that thing with you," she said, gesturing behind her, where a small backpack lay next to Tiger. "You won't pass through security with it."

"Understood," Tiger said. "We'll ditch it when we're done with it."

"Shame having to toss it," Dylan added.

"Yeah, but there won't be any time to store it somewhere safe," Tiger said. "The moment we use it, we'll only have so long before Polo gets wind of what's happening. We have to get to him before that, or he's in the wind, if he values his life and his freedom."

Dylan nodded. He knew what time constraints they were under. "All right." He pointed to the next street corner. "Let's get out here."

"It's still a few blocks to the White House," Zara replied.

"We'll walk from here. You need to get to your office on time so nobody suspects a thing."

Zara pulled the car to the curb and stopped. "Good luck."

Dylan leaned over to her and kissed her. "Be careful. If anything unexpected happens, send me a message."

Zara nodded, and Dylan exited the car. Tiger already stood on the sidewalk, a small backpack slung over one shoulder. As Zara merged back into traffic, he joined Tiger, and they started walking toward the White House. Dylan looked at his wristwatch. They were cutting it close. During rush hour traffic it had taken them longer to get here than he'd estimated.

"Let's pick up the pace," he said.

Tiger started walking faster, and they both hurried along without running. They were wearing business suits, which would make it easier to blend in with the people at the Capitol later, but would throw suspicion on them if they jogged outright.

"Fuck!" Tiger hissed as they were coming around a corner. "Damn tourists."

Dylan saw them too. Dozens if not hundreds of people crowded along the White House fence on E Street from where they had a perfect view of the South Lawn. It was evident that the tourists were taking this opportunity to take pictures of Marine One. There was no way they could activate their device from here.

"Chopper's already landed," Tiger pointed out, even though Dylan could see it too.

At best they had five minutes left until it would take off.

"This way," Dylan said, ushering Tiger to the right where the road made a bend, wrapping around the east side of the property. "I think we might have better access from up there."

They hurried past the crowd. It thinned almost immediately, since directly behind that part of the fence tall trees and thick bushes obstructed the view to the White House and the South Lawn. To their right, across the street, there were trees too, and Dylan knew that the General William Tecumseh Sherman Monument was located behind those trees. As the curve straightened, they reached a spot where a heavily guarded access road provided entry onto the White House grounds. Instinctively, they both slowed their pace and crossed the road. Only a few yards north of it, bushes and trees rose to their left. But between them, there was a small spot along the fence that offered a direct view of the spot where Marine One was sitting.

"This is it," Dylan said and glanced around. They were hidden from the guards at the gate, and while there were cars passing them, the trees along the street provided some cover.

Tiger turned his back to the street and opened his backpack. The device he pulled from it was no larger than a loaf of bread and weighed only two pounds. He powered it up.

"I only see one chopper," Tiger said with a sideways look at him.

"The decoys may be taking off from somewhere else, and join Marine One once in the air. I don't think we'll have to worry about that now. We'll be able to see POTUS and the VP get into this one. We only need to stop this one from taking off."

Tiger nodded. "All right."

"Do you have a signal?" Dylan asked, while he alternately watched the road behind them and the helicopter in front of the White House.

"Not yet." Tiger sounded tense. "Damn it, Fox," he

whispered into his earpiece. "I powered it up. Where's the signal?"

Dylan could hear Fox's response in his own earpiece.

"Thirty seconds."

"Fuck!" Dylan cursed and pointed to Marine One. He spotted several men in dark suits emerge from the White House. This could only mean one thing. "They're already getting on the chopper."

"Fox, get a move on," Tiger demanded. "We've gotta take it down before they lift off."

"Not helping," Fox admonished.

Anxious, Dylan watched the helicopter and noticed, judging by the noise, that the rotor blades were spinning faster. "The chopper is about to take off."

Marine One was suddenly moving up by a few feet.

"Now!" Fox's command was accompanied by a beeping sound coming from the device in Tiger's hands.

Tiger pressed a button, and the beeping stopped. They both stared at the chopper, which suddenly lost height and landed back on the ground, its rotor blades slowing, and the sound of the engine cutting out.

Dylan sighed in relief. "The electromagnetic pulse worked. The chopper is disabled."

To his surprise, Fox's voice came through the earpiece. "Don't sound so skeptical. Of course it worked."

"Why are the comms not down? Shouldn't the EMP have disabled them too?"

"No, most cell phones and smaller electronic devices still work."

"Good."

Meanwhile, Dylan watched as secret service agents surrounded the helicopter, weapons drawn, while the president and the VP were rushed into the building. By the looks of it, the drop of a few feet hadn't caused any injuries to the passengers.

Tiger was already wiping his fingerprints off the EMP device and shoved it back into the backpack. "Let's get rid of this."

While Dylan and Tiger crossed the street to get away from the White House, Fox spoke again.

"Guys, I'm handing communications over to Michelle."

"What's going on?" Dylan asked concerned.

"We picked up something on the surveillance of Smith's house in Fort Washington. I've gotta get over there. Something is going on."

"But you're needed if we need any technical help," Dylan protested.

"Michelle is more than capable of doing what I do, if not more so. Besides, according to my doomsday vision, I'm at Smith's house on the Potomac, trying to stop a countdown. I need to go there. There's a chance that the trigger for the bomb is there."

"Fine," Dylan said. "But you can't go alone."

"Don't worry, I'm taking Yankee as backup."

"You should take Ace too," Tiger suggested. "Don't underestimate Smith. He's probably not alone. He might have one of his goons there to protect him."

"Can't do. Ace has to stay at the mansion. Phoebe just went into labor."

"Fuck!" Dylan cursed. "Bad timing."

"Yeah, but Lilly and Olivia will help with the delivery. It leaves us a little short on manpower, but it can't be helped."

Dylan nodded to himself. "We'll make do."

"Signing off," Fox announced.

"Good luck!" Tiger said.

"I'm taking over comms," Michelle said through the earpiece. "Don't worry, boys, I'm keeping an eye on everything. You're in good hands."

"Appreciate it, Michelle."

"And don't forget to remove your earpieces before you go

through security at the Senate building, or you might look suspicious," she reminded them.

"Got it," Dylan said. "We'll check in later."

"Roger that."

Dylan nodded to Tiger as they passed a trashcan. With a quick glance around them to make sure they weren't being watched, Tiger dumped the backpack, and they continued walking.

20

Zara had arrived at her office in the Dirksen Senate office building on time. Clara, as well as the senator, had arrived before her, and Nicky and Ben had shown up a few minutes later. She'd made a point of mentioning that she'd bitten on something hard the night before, and that her tooth was still aching this morning. On and off during the morning, she faked pain when she drank hot coffee, and Clara had looked at her with compassion.

She glanced at her cell phone when she felt it vibrate. It was the signal that Dylan and Tiger were only ten minutes away from the building. Time to finalize her excuse to leave the office.

Zara took another sip from her coffee. She pulled a painful grimace and hissed. "Ouch!"

"Maybe you should go to the dentist," Clara suggested.

She pressed her hand against her cheek. "Maybe you're right." She lifted her cell and scrolled to Dylan's number. "I hope they can squeeze me in. They're always so busy."

Zara tapped on Dylan's number and brought the cell phone to her ear. When Dylan answered it, she said, "Oh, hello, Tanja, uhm, this is Zara Richardson. I wonder whether you could squeeze me in with Dr. Brown. I bit on something last night, and I think I might have cracked my tooth. And now I'm in a lot of pain." She paused.

"We're almost there," Dylan said. "All went well. The chopper is disabled."

"Oh, good!" she said cheerfully. "I'll leave right away. Thank you so much! I appreciate it."

She disconnected the call, shoved her cell phone into her handbag, grabbed her jacket, and rose. "They said he can take me if I get over there right away."

"Good," Clara said with a smile. "We'll see you later." She tilted her head in the direction of the senator's office door, which was closed. "I'll let him know. And call or text if you think you won't make it back in today."

"Of course, Clara, thanks."

Zara rushed out the door and pulled it shut behind her. She slipped into her jacket, arranged her staff badge so it was easily visible, and walked to the elevators. Earlier she'd already arranged for visitor passes for Dylan and Tiger, using the fake names they had provided her with. Dylan had assured her that the fake IDs that went with the names were foolproof thanks to Fox's IT skills and the high-quality printer at the mansion. She'd looked at the IDs herself the previous night, and had been surprised at how real they looked, watermarks and all.

Nevertheless, she was nervous as she waited in the foyer just a few yards away from the metal detector and the security desk when she finally saw Dylan and Tiger go through security. When the security guard checked their IDs against the register of visitors, Zara approached.

"Oh, there they are," she said cheerfully. She waved her staff badge at the security guard and addressed Dylan and Tiger, "Gentlemen, the senator is already expecting you."

The guard nodded. "I was about to call your office. You saved me a phone call."

She acknowledged his words with a smile. "Thanks."

Zara turned on her heel and motioned Dylan and Tiger to follow her. Instead of turning to the elevators, she turned in the other direction toward the Senate's own mini-subway system, which connected all three Senate buildings with the Capitol. There would be no more security checks from here on out. However, that didn't mean they didn't have to be careful.

As they reached the escalators that led down to the monorail track, Zara looked at Dylan. "We're not taking the rail."

"Why not?" he asked just as quietly.

"Because it gives people a chance to look at us for too long," she said. "It's better if we walk down the tunnel."

Dylan opened his mouth to say something, but Tiger spoke first. "And that's not suspicious?"

She shook her head. "Many of the staffers and even the senators walk to get a little exercise when they're not in a hurry. Nobody will take any notice of us."

"Us?" Dylan finally asked. "You're not coming with us. It's too dangerous."

"You can't go without me."

Dylan took her arm. "That wasn't the deal. We agreed that you'd get us inside. But there was no discussion of you coming with us."

"You don't have a choice. Visitors can only move around within the Capitol complex if they're accompanied by a representative or a staff member."

He narrowed his eyes. "You knew that. Yet you let me believe this entire time that Tiger and I would go in alone?"

Zara started walking along the tunnel, and Dylan and Tiger kept pace with her. "Of course I did. Otherwise, you would have never agreed to let me help you get in. If the Speaker is really behind this, then the only way to get to him is with my help. I know where his office is located, and the best way to get there without being seen by too many people."

Dylan grunted, and she could hear his frustration in his tone. But there was no way in hell she would let him go into the Capitol without her. If he and Tiger got stopped by security personnel realizing that they were unaccompanied, they would be detained.

"She's got a point," Tiger said in a low voice.

"Of course she's got a point," Dylan said with a sideways glance at her. "That's what makes it so infuriating."

Zara shrugged. "Get used to it. You really think that after what you told me over the last two days, I'd let you take any more risks than you are already taking?"

"I'm the one who's trained to take risks, not you."

"Yeah, well, I've gotten a crash course. Live with it!"

He grunted again, but didn't protest any further. As they walked the approximately quarter-mile long tunnel, they encountered only a handful of people coming from the Capitol. Nobody took any notice of them. Two trains drove past them in the time it took them to reach the foyer that opened up to the escalators that led to the first floor of the Senate side of the Capitol building.

One of the subway trains that had just passed them, had stopped there, and senators and staff members alighted. They were instantly surrounded by a throng of reporters sticking recording devices in their faces, peppering them with probing questions. The journalists took no notice of her and her companions, which made it easy to pass by them and get onto the escalators without delay. They reached the main floor of the Capitol building within a few short moments. It was unusually busy here, and she wondered whether the news that Marine One had been disabled had already made the rounds.

"We're on the Senate side of the Capitol building now," Zara explained with a look at Dylan and Tiger."

"How far to the Speaker's office?" Dylan asked.

"He has two offices; the formal one is in the House Chamber

in the south wing. But this time of day, he's most likely in the other office, the one just off the Rotunda. Follow me. And look like you belong here."

As they walked through the halls of power, the corridors where many a political alliance or policy were shaped, and the public areas where tourists admired the architectural beauty of the old building, Zara couldn't help but wonder how somebody could be so evil as to want to destroy this symbol of democracy. So many priceless and irreplaceable statues, paintings, and other artifacts adorned every hall they passed through, and the thought that all this could be destroyed if Polo wasn't stopped, made her sick. Inside these walls, history came alive for generation after generation to learn from and to cherish.

"It's beautiful," Tiger said next to her.

"Your first time?" she asked in a low voice.

He nodded.

"I hope all this can be saved," she mused.

To her left, Dylan touched her arm lightly, making her look at him. "We'll do everything in our power."

She gave him a smile, awareness traveling through her. The explosion in Dylan's vision could take place anytime. They were only a few yards away from the Speaker's office, the plaque of which Dylan had seen in the rubble. She tried to shake off the morbid thoughts, and flashed her badge at the guard at the entrance to the hallway that led to the Speaker's office. He was there to make sure that no tourists from the guided tours wandered off. With a nod, he waved them through. The first hurdle was behind them.

Zara took a steadying breath, every step bringing them closer to the Speaker's office. But what would they do once inside? They hadn't really discussed that, at least not in her presence. A staff member would most likely call security once they realized that the three of them had no official business with the Speaker of the House.

As they stopped a few feet away from the door to the Speaker's office, Zara turned to Dylan and Tiger. "What now? What are we gonna say to them when we're inside?"

"Let that be our problem. Stay outside. You work here. If something goes wrong, we don't want them to be able to identify you as being part of this."

Zara rolled her eyes and huffed. "Well, you're changing your tune like a flag in the wind. Didn't you say that you wouldn't leave my side if I ever got near the Capitol? Well, we're *inside* the Capitol. And now, you want me to wait here on my own?"

Dylan ran a hand through his hair, before letting out a breath. "You know you'll never be able to work here again if it all goes wrong."

She shrugged. "I don't like my job that much anyway."

"All right then. But you're staying behind us. Once we're inside, lock the door so nobody else can get in. Understood?"

"Understood."

He pulled his earpiece from his pocket and popped it back into his ear. When he tapped it, he cringed. "Only static. How about yours, Tiger?"

Tiger shook his head. "Same. Maybe there's too much interference here. We'll do without."

"All right." He nodded at Tiger. "I'm ready when you are."

"I've been ready for a long time, buddy."

21

———

P olo stared at the TV screen in his office. The plane carrying the coffin with the body of David Grossman, the VP's son, was scheduled to land shortly, yet POTUS and the VP weren't waiting on the tarmac yet. Something wasn't right. Marine One should have landed ten minutes ago at the latest. The reporter covering the event continued to speculate that delays like this were normal, and the arrival of the VP was imminent.

Polo continued watching the screen, becoming more impatient by the second. Perspiration began to accumulate on his brow, and he wiped it away with a tissue, then tossed it in the trash, but missed the basket. Everything hinged on this. Where the fuck were the president and the vice president? What was keeping them? His cell phone lay on his desk, and the app that would detonate the bomb at Joint Base Andrews was flashing at him.

Detonate? a red button blinked.

All of a sudden, the female reporter on the monitor pressed a finger to her earpiece, listening intently. At the same time, a red breaking news banner scrolled across the bottom of the screen.

"We've just received word that there's been an incident

involving Marine One."

Fuck!

Polo read the banner, which was scrolling far too slowly.

President and VP rushed to White House bunker after Marine One disabled during takeoff.

His insides churning with disbelief and fury, Polo turned up the sound as the reporter continued, "According to eyewitness reports, Marine One carrying President Mansfield and Vice President Grossman, was downed seconds after lifting off from the South Lawn. There is no word yet on any injuries or what or who caused this incident." She pressed on her earpiece again. "Hold on, we're getting more information." She nodded, then looked into the camera again, "We have a video recording from a tourist who was outside the fence of the White House when the incident happened."

A second later, the screen switched to a video clearly made with a cell phone camera. It showed Marine One lifting off, but not getting higher than a few feet, before it set down in one bumpy movement, the sound of its motor dying instantly, and the rotor blades turning slower. Within seconds, the chopper was surrounded by Secret Service personnel.

"As you may be able to see," the reporter said over the video, "the drop was only three to five feet, and there doesn't seem to be any damage to the helicopter itself. We can't see whether the president or the vice president were injured, because the helicopter is blocking our view of them exiting Marine One."

"Fuck!" Polo hissed, pounding his fist on his desk in frustration, making a few sheets of paper flutter.

With his remote control, he rewound the TV to the point where the chopper was lifting off, then setting down hard. He wasn't stupid. This was no regular technical glitch or malfunction. He'd seen this before. This sudden disabling of a large vessel with lots of electronics could only be achieved with an electromagnetic pulse. Somebody in the vicinity of the South

Lawn had sent an EMP to prevent Marine One from taking the president and the vice president to Joint Base Andrews. What was happening because of it was instantly clear: both passengers would already be in the bunker underneath the White House, out of his reach.

He wanted to scream, but there was no time to let out his frustration. They were onto him. How, he didn't know, and right now it didn't matter much. He had to act quickly. Because if they knew that he'd wanted to kill the president and the VP by detonating the bomb hidden in the coffin, they might soon figure out how to track him, no matter how careful he'd been.

He'd worked on this for months, for years, painstakingly putting every piece of the puzzle in place so that when the first domino fell, everything else would follow. For all he knew, one of the ex-Stargate agents had had a premonition of this event, and maybe of him too.

Right now, all he could do was to save what could be saved, and regroup later. He snatched his jacket, his keys, cell phone, and wallet, then grabbed his briefcase from below his desk, and cast a last look at his desk. There were no incriminating papers in his office. But there was another place where he'd hidden his most prized possession. Without it, he would never be able to try again. It was paramount that he collected the data that had allowed him to get as far as he had. If he hurried, he would make it.

By the time the Stargate agents knew who he was, he would be long gone. After all, he was much smarter than all of them together. He would get his revenge, maybe not today, but he could be patient. Tomorrow was another day. In the end, he'd be victorious, and nobody would ever stop him again.

Polo marched to the door and put his hand on the doorknob, before casting another look at everything this office signified in his life's work. He would be back, in one form or another. This wasn't the end, not by a long shot.

22

Dylan opened the door to the Speaker's office suite and entered swiftly, Tiger and Zara on his heels. He heard the soft click of Zara flipping the deadbolt. Quickly, he assessed the layout of the suite and the situation. There were several doors, two to the right, and another one to the left. Five people were present, three women, all of them sitting at their desks, and two men, one of whom was coming through a door from the right, carrying a stack of files, while the other man stood behind one of the women and looked over her shoulder into the computer monitor.

One of the women looked up as they approached. She raised her eyebrows, while she glanced at her computer screen as if checking something.

"Yes?" she asked, her tone curt, indicating she was busy or preoccupied with something else.

"We're here to see Speaker Johnson," Dylan said and stopped in front of her desk.

From the corner of his eye, he could see that Tiger had taken up a strategic point in the room so nobody would be able to get past him. Zara had remained at the door.

"He doesn't have any appointments on his calendar for now," she said just as curtly. She dropped her gaze to the visitor badge on his suit. "Mr. Smith-Bancroft."

Dylan had chosen the name—and Fox had forged a driver's license for it—because it would indicate to Polo that the jig was up. He leaned in. "Ma'am, I'm a personal friend of Speaker Johnson. He always has time for me."

When she glanced at the door to Dylan's left, he added, "No need to announce me, I'll just go in."

She quickly jumped up. "You can't go in there!"

Her words alerted the other staff members.

"I'm calling security," one of the men announced.

"I wouldn't do that," Tiger advised, his voice sounding menacing. "Step away from your desks, and lady, drop that phone."

One of the women shrieked, when Tiger lunged at her, while Dylan quickly approached one of the two men, and pressed him against a filing cabinet.

"Don't be a hero, buddy," he warned.

The man trembled, clearly afraid of physical violence.

"And don't even think about pressing the panic button," Zara interrupted, approaching too.

He wasn't pleased that Zara wasn't staying near the door like they'd discussed. But he had no time to scold her for disobeying his orders right now.

"Now everybody, behave. Nobody gets hurt as long as I get to see the Speaker." Dylan narrowed his eyes at the man in his grip, before releasing him. "Tiger, make sure they comply."

"Oh, I'm on it."

With three more steps, Dylan was at the door to the Speaker's office and ripped it open. He almost collided with him. It appeared that the Speaker had heard the commotion in his ante office and was coming to investigate. Dylan instantly noticed that Johnson looked out of shape. No matter the training he'd previously had, he would be easy to defeat in hand-to-hand combat.

"What's going on here?" Johnson asked with a raised voice. "Jennifer? What are these people doing here? Call security!"

"Not gonna happen," Dylan said.

"Who are you?"

"He said his name was Smith-Bancroft," the woman who'd confronted Dylan said from across the room.

Dylan looked straight at Johnson. "Yes, you've heard right, Polo. Smith-Bancroft. I know these names mean something to you. Or did you think that you could get away with this?"

Confused and annoyed, Johnson stared at him. "I'm the Speaker of the House, and I demand that you leave my office, or you will be prosecuted to the fullest extent of the law! Damn it! Somebody call security!"

There'd been no sign of recognition in Johnson's eyes when he'd dropped the three names: Polo, Bancroft, and Smith. Nobody could bluff that well. Nobody but a psychopath.

Dylan pushed him back with such force that Johnson tumbled against his desk. "Stay there! Where's your cell phone?"

Intimidated, Johnson pointed to a spot behind him on the desk. Dylan spotted the cell phone there, and snatched it. "Unlock it."

"How dare you?" Johnson spat.

Dylan went nose to nose with him. "I dare because I'm not gonna let you kill the president and the vice president so you can complete your evil plan!" He grunted in displeasure. "Now tell me how you're triggering the bomb."

Johnson gasped, and the people in the office behind him made similar sounds. "Bomb?" He motioned to the TV in his office. "There was a bomb on Marine One?"

Dylan drew back a few inches. The man was the best actor he'd ever seen, because the other possibility—that they had the wrong man—wasn't acceptable. "Fine! You wanna play hardball. I'll find the trigger myself."

He pulled out his cell phone and navigated to the app that Fox had installed earlier and activated it. A low steady beeping sound came from his cell phone. "This will pick up any device sending or receiving a signal." Then he called out toward the door, "Zara, Tiger, collect all cell phones and anything else that looks like it could be used to trigger a bomb."

"On it," Tiger answered.

Meanwhile, Dylan walked around the office, sweeping his cellphone over the desk, beneath it, inside of drawers, on the chairs, over the surfaces of every piece of furniture. He switched off the TV and unplugged it, then swept the area around the TV. The steady beeping sound continued.

He moved to the other side of the large room, where built-in closets framed a large painting, when the beeping sound suddenly intensified.

"Got something," he called out to Tiger. Then he addressed the Speaker, "What's in there?"

"Files."

When Dylan reached for the cabinet door, Johnson complained, "That's confidential records. Some of them are classified! You don't have the clearance—"

Dylan ripped the cabinet open and froze. At the same time, alerted by footsteps, he whipped his head to find Johnson only a few feet away from him, outrage coloring his face. Within a millisecond, his facial expression turned to panic.

"Oh my God!" The Speaker stared at the contents of the closet. "Is that a bomb?"

"Yeah."

And now that he was physically close to James Johnson, he realized something that he hadn't noticed when he'd first encountered him, maybe because his nape had still been tingling due to Tiger being close to him. But now, Tiger was in another room with a wall between them, and all he could sense coming from the Speaker was—in fact—nothing at all. There was no familiar tingling identifying Speaker Johnson as a precognitive. He wasn't Polo.

"Tiger," Dylan called out toward the open door. "There's a bomb in the Speaker's office."

"What?" Tiger replied, his voice full of disbelief. "Are you fucking with me?"

Tiger suddenly appeared in the door frame, and Dylan stepped aside so he could see the bomb hidden in the closet.

"Fuck!" Tiger hissed and looked over his shoulder. "You, Ma'am, call the bomb squad, now! And somebody call security to evacuate the Capitol."

Scared shrieks came from the employees.

Dylan crouched down to inspect the bomb closely, but this wasn't his field of expertise.

"How did you know there was a bomb in my office?" the Speaker asked.

"I didn't. I thought you had a trigger to the bomb that's meant to kill the president and the vice president."

"Me? I would never! Who the hell would make such an allegation?" Johnson's voice broke. "Did you plant this? Who did this? Who wants me dead?"

Dylan rose. "I can't diffuse the bomb. I think it has a remote detonator." He nodded at the Speaker. "I was wrong about you. You're not the man I thought you were. But you're in danger. I advise you to leave with your staff right now. You need to be in a bunker in case the bomb squad can't diffuse this bomb. Go!"

The Speaker hurried into the other room, yelling orders at his staff. Everybody was scrambling to get their phones, handbags, and briefcases as they rushed to the door.

Zara stood next to Tiger, trembling. Their eyes met. He knew what she was thinking. This was what he'd seen. But he wouldn't let it come to that.

"Speaker Johnson isn't Polo. We've got the wrong guy."

"The wrong James Johnson? Fuck!" Tiger cursed. "And somebody plants a bomb in his office? That can only mean one thing."

Dylan nodded. By now, all staff members had emptied out of the office suite. He pointed to the door, indicating that they should be leaving too. "Somebody wants him dead too." He looked at Zara, whose forehead was furrowed. "Zara, tell me: who will be president if the Speaker dies too?"

Her eyes widened. "The president pro tempore of the Senate."

"And who's that?" Dylan asked as he took her arm and they exited into the hallway, Tiger flanking them.

"James Johnson."

Dylan cast her a sideways look while he steered Zara down the corridor to where they'd come from. "No. Can't be. He's the Speaker. And we've already established that he's not Polo. He's not a precognitive."

Zara stopped and grabbed his arm, forcing him to stop too and turn to her. "What?"

"Senator James Johnson is the president pro tempore. He's the senator I work for."

"There is another James Johnson in the Capitol?" Dylan asked, stunned.

"Yes. He's been a senator for only a month. He was appointed by the Governor of Idaho after his father, the older Senator Johnson died suddenly."

Dylan exchanged a look with Tiger. "Is it possible?"

Tiger addressed Zara directly, "I thought the president pro tempore is generally the oldest serving member of the Senate. So if he's only been in office for a month... You must be wrong."

She shook her head. "His father was president pro tempore. He basically inherited the position, and because it's so close to summer recess, and a couple of the senators of the majority party were out sick, they haven't been able to hold a vote for it yet, or there would have been a danger of the minority party electing their own candidate to the position." Zara spoke fast, rushing to get the information across.

"Fuck!" Dylan cursed. "It all fits! Why didn't you tell me that there was another James Johnson here?"

Zara huffed. "Because I had no idea that your suspect was a James Johnson. You only ever called him Polo. How was I supposed to know?"

Dylan squeezed her shoulder. "I'm sorry. It's not your fault. But we have to act fast now. Where is Senator Johnson?"

She looked at her watch. "I'm not sure. He might still be in the office in the Dirkson building." She pulled out her cell phone. "I'm gonna ask my colleagues." She tapped on a contact, and let it ring.

Simultaneously, a deafening alarm sounded in the Capitol. Moments later, a voice coming through the loudspeaker made an announcement. *"This is not a test. Please evacuate the Capitol. This is not a test. Please evacuate the Capitol."*

He couldn't hear Zara's conversation with her colleague. More and more people were coming out of their offices and rushing toward the exits, while the announcement was repeated over and over. Finally, Zara ended her call and shoved her cell phone into her handbag.

"He's not in the Senate building anymore. He told them that he'd forgotten a private appointment, and had to run out maybe fifteen minutes after I left the office."

Dylan exchanged a look with Tiger. "He figured out that we foiled his plan to kill the president and the VP. I saw on the TV in the Speaker's office that the news reports were already in that Marine One was disabled, and that the president and the VP were taken to the bunker underneath the White House. He must have realized that we're on his tail."

"Makes sense," Tiger agreed. "So where would he go? Is he gonna hide somewhere, or is he gonna run?"

"He's gonna go wherever he's hidden the data of the brain scans. He can't let that fall into our hands," Dylan mused. "He would have hidden it close-by in case of an emergency like this. Not in his office, where we'd find it once we knew his identity, and not at his home, because who knows how long it would take him to get there from his office."

"Yes, somewhere close. Somewhere in the Capitol," Zara echoed and took Dylan's hand.

"Which is being evacuated right now," Dylan said with a shake of his head. "We can't stay here."

"He won't trigger the bomb as long as he's still in the Capitol himself. We're safe for now."

He met her gaze. "The Capitol is huge. Where would we even begin?"

"I know where. Follow me," Zara said confidently.

Dylan took in a deep breath, and allowed her to usher him and Tiger down another corridor. He could only hope that Zara was right. And that Polo was still in the building.

He addressed Tiger, "Call Fox and Yankee, and update them. I'm calling Michelle." He pulled his cell phone from his pocket and tapped on the main number for the mansion. Michelle picked up almost instantly.

23

"Alarm is disabled," Fox whispered.

Yankee nodded. They were outside of John Bancroft's house in Fort Washington, disguised as workers from the power company so none of Bancroft's neighbors would find it suspicious that they were working on the fuse box and the cables that brought internet and phone service to the property. They were both wearing gloves so as not to leave any fingerprints.

"Okay," Yankee whispered back. "Time to pick the lock."

"Hurry," Fox advised. "If he checks his camera feeds frequently, he'll realize pretty quickly that it's been disabled."

"I'm on it," he confirmed, while he already went to work on the side door that led into the three-car garage. It didn't take long. The lock was flimsy at best. "Here you go."

Yankee pressed down on the door handle and pushed the door slowly, not wanting to hit any obstacles that would cause noise and therefore alert Bancroft to their arrival. He peered inside the garage, and saw that an SUV was parked there. It was the same one they'd followed months earlier to figure out who

Bancroft—whom they only knew as Mr. Smith back then—was, and where he worked.

Seeing that the garage was otherwise empty, Yankee waved Fox to follow him. They entered the garage, and Fox closed the door behind them quietly. Yankee walked toward the door that led into the house, and listened intently. He heard a female voice, but couldn't make out the words. Did Bancroft have a visitor? There'd been no cars in the driveway.

"You hear that?" he whispered to Fox.

For a few moments, they both remained silent, when Yankee could suddenly hear a few musical notes that he recognized as the introduction to a TV news program.

"He's watching TV," Fox confirmed.

Yankee drew his gun. Fox already held his in his hand. "Let's do this."

Yankee eased the door open slowly, and the sound coming from the TV grew louder. It came from the left. He made a sign to Fox, then opened the door fully and entered the short hallway that opened up to a large kitchen. The remnants of a breakfast— a dirty plate and bowl, a half-empty French press, butter, and a jar of jam—was on the kitchen island together with a newspaper. The kitchen was otherwise empty.

Yankee tipped his head in the direction of the sound of the TV. What he knew from the blueprints Fox had been able to pull from the city records, he was aware that there were two doors leading into the living room, as well as one leading onto a terrace that overlooked the Potomac.

Fox pointed to a door at the other end of the kitchen, indicating that he would approach the living room from the other side. Yankee nodded wordlessly, and tiptoed toward the half-open door leading into the living room, while Fox continued straight. Fox lifted his hand, spreading his five fingers to indicate a countdown. Yankee understood. He was to give Fox five seconds to get into position.

At the door to the living room, Yankee waited while he scanned as much as he could from his vantage point. He saw part of the TV, where a news program was reporting that the president and VP were taken to the bunker underneath the White House, and speculations were rife as to what exactly had taken down Marine One.

There was a large sectional and two large armchairs in front of the TV, but Yankee couldn't see if anybody sat on the sectional. The backrest was high enough to hide anyone if the person was slouching.

The five seconds were up, and Yankee ripped the door open wider and burst into the room. Fox did the same from the other door. Like he'd learned in the army and as a CIA agent, Yankee surveyed every corner, gun drawn. But the room was empty. He made another step, and almost lost his balance. He looked down at his feet, and noticed that an indoor golf mat lay along the wall, and several white golf balls were strewn about. A putter leaned against the armrest of an armchair. He quickly surveyed the rest of the room. To his right, along the wall opposite the TV, was a large sideboard made of decorative wrought iron and colored glass. The monstrosity fit perfectly with the heavy curtains adorned with tassels and the flower-heavy wallpaper covering the walls. It looked like he'd stepped into the 1960s.

Yankee looked at Fox, when he suddenly heard a toilet flush in the distance.

He hurried to the origin of the sound, a powder room underneath the stairs leading to the second floor. He pointed his gun at the door, and Fox joined him just as the door was opened, and Bancroft emerged.

Recognition lit up in his eyes and a shocked gasp rolled over his lips. He stepped back and tried to shut the door in Yankee's face, but the powder room was small, and there wasn't much space to maneuver. One push against Bancroft's chest, and the idiot landed on the toilet.

"Mr. Smith," Yankee said, drawing out his words to prolong the pleasure of finally capturing the asshole who'd sent assassins after him and his brethren—and had ordered Lilly's death too. "We finally meet again."

"You're confusing me with somebody. My name is Bancroft," the weasel claimed, his body trembling visibly.

"I would never forget the face of the asshole who tried to kill Lilly," Yankee swore.

Resignation flickered in Bancroft's eyes now. He knew he'd lost.

His gun still in his right hand, Yankee grabbed Bancroft's collar with his left and pulled him up. When he tried to shake off his grip, Yankee put his gun underneath Bancroft's chin and growled.

"It'll be messy, but I don't mind," he said. "It's not like I have to clean up here after you."

The warning was clear even to the loser in his grip. Bancroft swallowed hard, and Yankee pressed the gun deeper into the soft flesh underneath his jaw and pulled him out of the small room, while he turned to Fox. "Frisk him!"

Fox patted him down, then shook his head. "No weapons."

"Let's have a look at what you've got, shall we?" Yankee asked, while he dragged him to the living room.

Fox snatched Bancroft's cell phone from the coffee table. He tapped on it. "It's locked."

"Right thumb," Yankee demanded as Fox stopped next to him and grabbed Bancroft's hand. Bancroft had no choice but to press his thumb on the cell phone to unlock it.

From the corner of his eye, Yankee watched as Fox connected a cable to the cell phone, and tapped on his own phone. It took only a few moments, before Fox shook his head and tossed Bancroft's cell phone back on the table.

"Nothing."

"Well, then we have to do it the old-fashioned way, won't

we?" Yankee said, looking straight at Bancroft, who's eyes widened in fear.

Before he could start with his interrogation, Fox pulled his cell phone from his pocket. "It's Tiger." Fox tapped on it and pressed it to his ear. "Yeah?"

Fox listened intently, his eyes widening, surprise registering on his face.

"What's wrong?" Yankee asked, instantly alarmed.

Fox lifted his hand. "No, we've already got Smith. We're about to interrogate him." A short pause, then Fox added, "Yeah, we'll sweep the house, just in case it's here." He disconnected the call.

"What happened?" Yankee asked, tossing Bancroft onto the sectional, while keeping a close eye on him, the gun still pointed at him.

"The Speaker isn't Jones."

"Fuck!" They'd gotten it wrong. They'd messed up, and now their chance of taking down Jones was practically nil. Because once Jones found out that he and his friends had gotten to Smith, he'd be in the wind.

"But they figured out who Jones really is. He's the next in line for the presidency after the Speaker: Senator James Johnson from Idaho. He's Polo. They found a bomb in the Speaker's office. Polo must have placed it there to get rid of the Speaker, so he'd become president."

The news was a revelation. "So we've got him?"

"Almost. The Capitol is being evacuated right now, but Tiger said they believe they know where he's hiding."

Yankee nodded. "Good. Then we just need to get on with our part of the job." He smiled at Bancroft. "Which brings me back to you."

Bancroft sank deeper into the sofa cushions, while Yankee leaned in. "I know nothing," Bancroft spat defiantly. "I didn't even know who Jones is. Had I had any idea, I would have—"

"You would have what?" Yankee challenged.

When Bancroft didn't say anything, Yankee added, "So, let's get down to business. Who's got the trigger for the bomb in the coffin?"

Bancroft's forehead furrowed. "What coffin?"

"The coffin that's carrying the VP's dead son," Yankee snapped.

Bancroft suddenly looked at the TV screen where the reporter was hypothesizing about what had brought down Marine One, when his facial expression changed as if the penny finally dropped. Had he really been so stupid as not to know what his boss had planned?

"Are you saying..." He shook his head. "He never told me! I'm not part of that. I was never told about any of that. I was just a small cog in the machine. Insignificant." He was babbling now, clearly trying to downplay his part in the scheme.

Yankee looked at Fox, who'd already pulled out a small device from his bag of tricks. "Start scanning the place, just in case he resists torture." Not that Bancroft looked like he could take a lot of pain, but even as a man working in CIA management, he would have had basic training.

"Torture? No, no, don't!" He lifted his hands. "I know nothing. You must believe me."

Fox wandered around the room, the device in his hand making a steady beeping sound.

"Must I? I don't think so." Yankee leaned over him and pressed his gun underneath Bancroft's chin again, driving it up into the soft tissue. "You don't give the orders here. Now tell me how the bomb in the coffin will be triggered."

"I don't know," Bancroft whimpered. "I don't know anything about a trigger. Or a bomb."

"I think he's telling the truth," Fox suddenly interrupted at the same time as his device began to emit a high-pitched sound.

Yankee looked over his shoulder, and saw Fox crouching

down in front of the fireplace. He couldn't see what Fox was inspecting. "What is it?"

Fox turned his head. "A bomb. With what looks like a timer."

Bancroft gasped, and Yankee turned back to him. "Looks like your boss is tying up loose ends."

"That fucker!" Bancroft choked out. "That's why he told me to stay home today. So he could kill me. I'm gonna nail his ass. He's not gonna get away with this!"

Yankee couldn't pity the man. He'd had it coming, and for all he cared, they could just tie him up here and let fate run its course. But he'd only ever killed in self-defense, or to prevent a catastrophe. After all these years of living on the run, he still had scruples. And they were rearing their head now.

"How much time do we have?" Yankee asked without looking back at Fox.

"Twenty-seven minutes."

24

Zara ushered Dylan and Tiger toward another set of stairs. "This way."

Moments earlier, Tiger had reported that Fox and Yankee had overpowered Bancroft at his home. The man who was working together with Senator Johnson wouldn't be able to detonate the bombs at the Capitol and in the coffin arriving at Joint Base Andrews, if he indeed had the trigger.

Dylan finally finished his call with Michelle, and shoved his cell phone back in his pocket. "The plane with the coffin just landed. I told Michelle to call in a bomb threat. We have no other choice. Polo might detonate it just out of spite if he knows that we thwarted his plan to kill the president and the VP."

"Good point," Tiger commented.

"You think he would do that? Detonate the bomb out of spite?" Zara asked, shivering at the thought of how evil Senator Johnson had to be to be capable of such a deed.

"I wouldn't put it past him. When I met him—"

"You met him? When?" Zara whipped her head to stare at Dylan, while they continued walking up the stairs, surprised at his claim.

"Yeah, when I was first recruited by the CIA. Frankly, the guy gave me the creeps."

"He always seemed pleasant in the office," she mused.

"Psychopaths learn to disguise their true nature. They can be very charming when they want to. They can fool a lot of people," Dylan answered.

The events of the past few days played in her head again. "When it was reported that the VP's son was badly injured in Afghanistan, he was the first to want to show his support for the VP, and he had us look into what kinds of presents, or flowers, or whatever we could send to convey that he cared."

She huffed. "Clearly, it was all an act!" Another thought ricocheted in her brain. She didn't really want to express it, but she felt she had to. "Do you think he's capable of killing his own father?"

Dylan met her gaze and held it for a second as they hurried along another corridor. "Wasn't his father quite old?"

"Yes, but he was healthy. He'd only just gotten his checkup from the Capitol physician, and there was nothing wrong with him. And a week later, he just dropped dead. His son was the first to claim it was his heart, and nobody contradicted him."

"Polo would have planned all this for a very long time, ever since he was dismissed from the Stargate program," Dylan said with a nod. "And it's entirely possible that he killed his father, timing his death in such a way that the vote for president pro tempore couldn't take place right away, making him automatically the third in line for the presidency. And with the data he's already collected for his quantum computer, he would have had some help in predicting what would happen if he did x, y, or z."

"That's terrible." Zara oriented herself, before pointing to a short corridor to her left. "This way."

"Where are you taking us?" Tiger asked from behind her.

"To his hideaway office."

"A hideaway office?" both Tiger and Dylan asked in unison.

"Yes, all senators have a private office that they can sneak off to if they want to work undisturbed. Some of them are huge, others feel more like a broom closet, and virtually nobody knows where they are. There are no signs on the doors, nothing."

"Then how do you know where Johnson's hideaway office is?" Dylan asked.

"His father showed it to me once," Zara explained, "when he needed help with carrying something. And his son would know about it too. He mentioned to me only a few days ago that he knows the Capitol like the back of his hand, because he visited his father often when he was a kid and a young adult. He would assume that none of his staff knows about the location of the hideaway office. It's the perfect place to hide something he doesn't want to be found, including himself."

She stopped in front of an indistinct door. They were on one of the upper floors of the rotunda. "This is it."

"Is this the only entrance?" Tiger asked, keeping his voice low, though it wouldn't be necessary. The alarm was still blaring in the building, and if Johnson was indeed in the hideaway office, he wouldn't hear them over the noise.

"Yes."

Dylan tested the door handle. "It's unlocked. Zara, step over there; Tiger, on three."

Zara watched the two as they looked at each other and counted silently. On three, Tiger ripped the door open, and Dylan rushed inside, Tiger hot on his heels. From her position in the hallway, she looked into the room, and realized instantly that Johnson wasn't there.

She joined Dylan and Tiger inside the shoebox-sized hideaway office. There was a round window like a porthole that let the sun in, making the room bright and warm. Several of the built-in cabinets stood open, and files and folders were strewn about the desk and the floor. A small metal suitcase no larger than a lunch box lay next to one of the open cabinets. There were several indentations in the foam-lined container. Indentations large enough for discs or external hard drives.

Dylan lifted the case from the floor and placed it on the small desk. "You were right, Zara. He kept the data discs hidden here where they were protected well, and close enough for him to access in an emergency. He beat us to it."

The disappointment in Dylan's voice was palpable. Tiger didn't look happy either.

"Damn," Zara cursed. "I should have gotten us here faster."

Dylan put a hand on her shoulder. "It's not your fault. Without you, we wouldn't even know who he is. So get those thoughts right out of your head, all right?"

She nodded reluctantly, wondering if there was anything else she could help them with. After all, of the three of them, she probably knew Johnson the best. She'd worked for him for a month. She knew some of his quirks and habits, some of his routines. Though she doubted that he would follow any of his routines today, given that he knew his plan had been thwarted—for now.

"Hawk, do you think he took the data to where the computer or the MRI machine is?" Tiger asked, rubbing the back of his neck. "I mean, if he wants to try again, he'll need what he's already built, right?"

Dylan nodded. "Yes, but Fox said that you guys have no lead on where he set up the new MRI machine after you all blew the one up that they'd put you in, right?"

"True, but that thing is big, and it takes a lot of juice to run it," Tiger added.

Zara listened up. Something Tiger had just said triggered something in her brain. But what was it?

"We'll have to get Fox or Michelle to hack into the utility company to see who's using a lot of electricity. Wasn't that how they found the other MRI machine in the first place? By checking for electricity usage?"

"I'll call Michelle," Tiger offered and pulled his cell phone from his pocket. "She can start checking any utility bills registered in the senator's name."

Zara slapped her palm to her forehead. "That's it!" Excitement coursed through her. "Now I remember."

"You remember what?" Dylan asked, looking straight at her, while Tiger waited too.

"The utility bill. A few days ago, I was going through the senator's mail, and I got this utility bill in his name, but it was for a property that wasn't on my list belonging to either him or his father. And the bill was pretty high. So I brought it to his attention, and asked him if I should pay it or not."

"And?" Tiger asked eagerly.

"Well, he said he needed to pay it from his private funds, and took it from me, even though I could have easily made the payment for him. Clara, my colleague, has checks for his private account, and normally prepares the checks for his signature."

Dylan leaned closer, excited now. "Do you remember the address?"

"Only the street, not the number."

Dylan and Tiger exchanged a look. "Call Michelle. Let's give her the street name, and she can check if anything on that street is registered in Johnson's name, and if that doesn't pan out, she can hack into the utility company's records and find any property on that street that has unusually high usage." He nodded at her. "How far from here is it?"

"Only about half a mile, but the streets will be clogged right now," she advised. "Everybody will be trying to get as far away from the Capitol as possible. It'll take too long to get my car out of the parking garage."

"We'll walk," Dylan suggested. "We have to assume that Johnson faces the same predicament. He has to get there too. I doubt he'll go back to fetch his car. It's too risky for him. He probably thinks that we have a person waiting there for him. He'll be on foot. And he can't be that far ahead of us."

"All right," Zara said and headed out the door. "Let's go. There's a faster way to get out of the building from here."

"Lead the way," Dylan said, and all three of them rushed through the corridor and down the next flight of stairs.

25

Ace hurried down the stairs. He had only minutes until Phoebe's next contraction, but he needed to check in with Michelle to see whether there was anything he needed to do. He entered the command center where Michelle was on the phone. She looked at him, and motioned him to approach.

"Okay, thanks Tiger, I'm on it," she said, before disconnecting the call.

"What's the latest?"

"Tiger and Hawk are still in the Capitol with Zara. Polo hid the discs with the brain scans in some hideaway office in the Capitol, but they got there too late. He's already taken them and got away."

"Fuck!" Earlier, Hawk had called in with the news that the Speaker of the House wasn't Polo as they'd suspected. Instead, the senator Zara worked for was the man they'd been looking for. And Zara had inside knowledge of where he might be hiding.

"But they have another lead. I've gotta check on an address in D.C., not too far from the Capitol. They think that's where he keeps the MRI machine—"

"Like the one we destroyed a few months ago?" Ace interrupted.

"Yep, looks like he's built another one. Apparently, Zara saw a utility bill that was extremely high." Michelle turned back to her computer. "I'd better get on it. They only have a partial address, but I should be able to narrow it down by the time they get close to it."

"Can I help you with anything?"

A loud cry of pain came from upstairs.

"No. I've got this. Go! Phoebe needs you. I'll use the speaker system if anything urgent comes up."

"All right. Thanks, Michelle."

Ace hurried out of the room and ran upstairs. In the master bedroom, Lilly and Olivia were busy making Phoebe comfortable. They had moved her onto a wide gurney with stirrups that Lilly had ordered from a medical supply company only a month earlier. She'd insisted that it would be easier for Phoebe to push with her feet in the stirrups than if she were lying in a bed. Ace could see now that Lilly had been right. Propped up against the backrest, both feet in the stirrups, Phoebe gripped one of Olivia's hands tightly.

Lilly sat on a low stool between Phoebe's legs. "The head's crowning."

Ace hurried to Phoebe's side, and put one arm around her back, while he took her hand. She looked at him, her hair wet from perspiration, her face red, and beads of sweat running down her gown.

"I'm here, baby," he murmured to her. "You can do this."

Before she could answer, another contraction made her scream, while Lilly ordered, "Push, push, push."

Ace felt Phoebe's hand grip his with such force that she almost crushed it, but he didn't care. He wished he could do more for her, but he didn't have any medical skills to take away her pain. All he could do was to be there for her.

"You're doing great, baby," he murmured to her, massaging her lower back like Lilly had shown him earlier.

For a moment, Phoebe breathed evenly, indicating that this contraction had reached its end. But the next one was only a minute away.

"Next time I'm having a cesarean, or at least an epidural," Phoebe swore, before her face contorted with pain.

"Breathe, breathe, breathe," Lilly demanded. "His head is coming." Lilly glanced up at Phoebe. "You're doing great, honey. Just a little bit longer. Push a little more. You can do it."

While Phoebe pushed again, grunting and cursing, Olivia moved to Lilly's side now, fresh linens in her hands, ready for the baby.

Ace couldn't help but admire all three women: Phoebe for never complaining that he hadn't brought her to a hospital, Lilly for practically learning a new-to-her medical discipline, and Olivia for being so willing to do whatever Lilly or Phoebe needed her to do.

Ace pressed a kiss on top of Phoebe's head. "I love you, Phoebe, I love you so much."

Again, Phoebe breathed rhythmically, while she leaned forward with the next contraction and pushed. This time, it looked more effortless than he'd observed before.

"I have the head," Lilly said, smiling up at Phoebe. "Just another push, and your little boy will be out."

Ace looked at Phoebe, and they locked eyes. Then she closed her eyes and pushed, her teeth clenched, her hand crushing his, while she gripped the gurney's guardrail with the other. A woosh of air releasing from her lungs followed.

"He's out!" Lilly cried out, and transferred the little bundle onto the soft cloth Olivia was holding out, crouched down next to Lilly. "Hold on, I've gotta clamp off the umbilical cord."

While Lilly and Olivia did what they needed to do, Ace

pressed his forehead to Phoebe's. "You did it. I'm so proud of you, baby."

The baby's crying finally bounced off the walls, and he couldn't remember ever having heard a more wonderful sound.

"We did it," Phoebe said breathlessly, and he pressed a kiss to her lips.

"*You* did it." Then he glanced at Lilly and Olivia. "And Lilly and Olivia. Thank you both so much."

Both smiled, and finally, with the umbilical cord severed, Olivia laid the baby on Phoebe's chest. "Say hello to your little baby boy. He's perfect."

Tears streamed down Phoebe's face, and Ace felt his own eyes well up with tears. He stroked over his son's head, feeling the dark fuzzy hair that felt as soft as down feathers. He was still full of blood and amniotic fluid, but it didn't matter. He was the most beautiful thing he'd ever seen in his life.

"Oh," Phoebe marveled as she took his tiny hand. "He's so perfect."

"And he's ours," Ace said and pressed a kiss on Phoebe's forehead.

"What will you name him?" Lilly asked.

"Henry," Phoebe said, and looked at Ace with a smile.

Ace nodded. It had been Phoebe's idea. "After my father." So he would always remember the man who'd given him everything, and made this life possible.

26

"Can you disable it?" Yankee asked.

Fox didn't look over his shoulder to where Yankee was watching Bancroft. Instead, he examined the mechanism of the bomb in the fireplace. He'd already removed the grill with the fake wood in front of it, so he could get better access to the explosive device.

"Not sure yet. It's not exactly my field of expertise," Fox confessed, even though he knew a few basic things about bombs.

"You probably know more than I do," Yankee claimed.

Fox flipped him the bird without turning around. "Just keep an eye on Bancroft."

"You've gotta let me go!" Bancroft cried out as if on cue. "None of you knows how to diffuse a bomb. That's pretty obvious. So, we've gotta leave, before this damn thing goes off."

"Yankee, tell him to shut it! I can't hear myself think," Fox said while he shone a tiny flashlight onto the bomb to figure out its mechanism. However, the bombmaker had been clever: he hadn't left many wires exposed, and the ones that were, were all the same color: black. That fact pissed him off. Apparently, Polo had expected that somebody would try to diffuse the bomb, and left as few clues to its design as possible.

"You heard my buddy," Yankee said with an icy undertone in his voice.

"Damn it," Bancroft complained, his voice getting louder. "Don't be so stupid! Nobody here has to die. Let's get out of here."

"Sit back down!" Yankee growled.

"I won't."

A thumping sound followed Bancroft's refusal, and Fox cast a quick look over his shoulder. Bancroft cowered on the sofa holding his jaw. It appeared that Yankee had punched hard enough for Bancroft to land back on his ass.

Fox tuned out the low grumbling coming from Bancroft and examined the bomb further, while he kept an eye on the countdown. Sixteen minutes to go till detonation.

"Can't you just take the bomb and toss it out into the river?" Yankee asked.

"I could, if only it hadn't been bolted down to the concrete floor of the fireplace. Somebody thought of everything." He shifted to get a better look at the back side of the device. "But maybe I can take off the casing to get to the inside."

"Do that," Yankee encouraged him.

It was easier said than done. While two of the screws that held the device together were located on the front, and thus easily accessible, from what he could see, the others were located in the back at an angle that was difficult to reach with a regular screwdriver. He had to improvise. The two screws on the front were easy to loosen, but even when he removed them, the casing still held together.

"I need a dime," Fox said with a glance over his shoulder.

"A dime?"

"Yeah, so I can turn the screws on the back, and hopefully remove the casing in one piece."

He watched as Yankee dug into his pockets, before shaking his head. "Don't have any." He glanced at Bancroft. "You keep change somewhere?"

"Yeah," Bancroft said, pointing across the room, where a built-in cabinet housed various porcelain statues and carvings. "There's a bowl in the middle drawer. I'll get it for you."

He already jumped up, but Yankee pushed him back into the cushions. "I'll get it. You stay put. For all I know you keep a gun in there."

Yankee turned his back to Bancroft and hurried to the cabinet. Fox glanced back at the timer on the bomb. "Fourteen minutes."

He heard Yankee pull at the drawer. "Fuck, it's locked."

Alarmed, Fox looked over his shoulder again, only to see a rapid movement from the corner of his eye. In his crouching position it took him an extra second to jump up and fully turn only to see that Bancroft had gotten up from the couch. He was now wielding a putter and swung it toward the approaching Yankee, hitting him in the side, making him crash into the coffee table.

"Fuck!" Fox cursed, and rushed toward Bancroft, while Yankee recovered from the unexpected attack and rose a couple of seconds later.

"Asshole," Yankee yelled and charged toward Bancroft from the other side, giving the bastard only one path toward the door. "Now I'm really gonna hurt you."

Tossing his golf club behind him as an obstacle for his pursuers, Bancroft rushed toward the door. He was only a few feet away from it, when his right leg suddenly kicked forward and upward, making him lose his balance. A golf ball hit the wall and bounced back. A panicked gasp burst from his lips as he used his arms as if they were rudders—to no avail. They didn't find purchase anywhere. Instead, his body twisted to the side, and as he tumbled backwards and released a desperate yelp, his head hit the corner of the iron-and-glass sideboard. The decorative figures on the glass surface fell over, and the glass cracked, while Bancroft landed on the wooden floor.

Yankee was at his side a second before Fox. Bancroft didn't move. Yankee put his fingers to his neck, but Fox didn't need to wait for him to check for a pulse. Blood was already pooling on the wooden floor.

Yankee removed his fingers from Bancroft's neck. "He's dead."

"Never realized how dangerous golf can be," Fox mused with a shrug. "Serves him right. It's not like he doesn't deserve it."

"My sentiments exactly," Yankee agreed.

"No point in diffusing the bomb now. We might as well have the whole place go up in smoke. Saves us from having to deal with the body. What do you say?"

"What are we still doing here?"

Together, they rushed to get out of the house, then walked back to their vehicle at normal speed in case any neighbors were watching. Luckily, Bancroft's house was located around a curve of the road, making it practically impossible for any neighbors to see who was coming and going. They hopped into the van and drove off.

Yankee stuck to the 25-mile speed limit in the residential neighborhood, while Fox looked at his watch. Any moment now, the bomb would go off.

A loud boom interrupted the silence in the car. Fox looked into the side mirror and saw a plume of smoke rise over the trees and bushes where Bancroft's house had stood.

"Well, better call the mansion to let them know that we're okay," Fox said and pulled out his cell phone.

"And that Bancroft is taken care of," Yankee added. "And we didn't even have to get our hands dirty."

"It's a win-win." The call connected, and Fox heard

Michelle's voice on the other line. "Hey, babe. Yankee and I are on our way back."

"And Bancroft? Did you get him?" she asked eagerly.

Fox exchanged a look with Yankee. "Well, the idiot practically did the job for us."

"Yeah," Yankee added, "too stupid to live."

27

"It's confirmed. This is the address," Dylan said, and slipped his cell phone back into his pocket.

He, Tiger, and Zara were across from a small two-story building that looked like an old house that had been converted to a commercial building. It looked unremarkable among the row of other similar buildings. Nobody would find it out of place. There was no doorbell, no sign or anything else outside that could identify the owner or occupier.

"What now?" Zara asked, standing close to him, her apprehension palpable.

"Wish we had guns," Tiger said, giving him a worried look.

"That wasn't an option, or we would have never gotten past security. It is what it is," Hawk said, then turned to Zara. "Tiger and I will pick the lock and go inside. You'll stay out here."

"But—"

"Don't." He pulled his cell phone out of his pocket and unlocked it. "Get your cell phone out."

Zara retrieved her cell phone, and a moment later it rang. She tapped on *answer*.

"Okay, I'll keep my cell phone in my pocket, so you can hear everything that's going on inside, but you'll need to put yours on mute, otherwise any sound might alert Polo to our presence."

"No problem." She tapped on her cell phone. "It's muted." She looked across the street, then up to the second floor, and Dylan followed her gaze. The blinds of the three windows overlooking the street were drawn. "What if he's already seen us?"

Dylan met her eyes. "Then we'd probably already be dead."

Zara put her arms around him and squeezed him tightly. "Be careful."

He nodded, and peeled himself out of her embrace, then crossed the narrow street with Tiger by his side. "How are your hand-to-hand combat skills?"

"Pretty good. Tai Chi, karate, jiujitsu, I've got us covered," Tiger replied with confidence.

"Good. All I learned was boxing."

"That's not a useless skill either."

"I suppose you didn't bring your lockpicks, did you?"

"Didn't wanna risk getting caught with them going through security."

"Well, guess we'll have to improvise." Dylan pulled out his wallet and removed the metal money clip holding the banknotes in place. "I need a second piece. You have one in your wallet?"

Tiger was already pulling out his wallet, and copied him. Within seconds they had two thin and long pieces of metal to use as makeshift lockpicks. Dylan went to work, and while it took a little longer to pick the lock with such crude tools, he managed it. Making eye contact with Tiger, he turned the knob, and eased the door open by an inch. There was a steady sound coming from the inside. It sounded like the humming of a machine like a refrigerator—or something bigger.

With another nod, Dylan swung the door open fully and entered the dark interior, Tiger on his heels. It was risky to enter this place without a weapon, but it was a calculated risk. Polo would have been without a weapon too, since he came straight from the Capitol. And they were only a few minutes behind him. With some luck, he hadn't had time to arm himself—unless of course, he kept a weapon at this property.

Dylan listened intently, and in the darkness, they moved farther into the house, following the humming sound. To their right, a door stood open, and inside the large space that appeared to have once been a sitting and dining room with pocket doors separating the two rooms, stood a large machine. It looked very similar to an MRI machine. He glanced around the room, but apart from the machine, a desk with computers, and other devices that looked like data storage, there wasn't much to see.

Tiger pointed to the machine and leaned in closer, whispering, "That's the same type of machine I was in. But it looks like the gurney is different. There used to be a helmet to lock your head in."

The machine was running, though Dylan couldn't tell whether it had been switched on only minutes earlier, or whether it ran on standby all the time. He approached the machine and looked at the desk and the tower that looked like a server. "Do you know what the discs look like? I can't see anything here."

"They are like external hard drives. Pretty big." Tiger let his eyes roam over the computers and the server, then shook his head. "They're not here. He might not be back. Maybe he stopped off somewhere."

"That's possible," Dylan said just as quietly so they wouldn't be overheard by anyone in the house, even though the sound of the machine drowned out his voice. "Let's check upstairs."

Tiger nodded. Together, they walked up the old staircase, aware of their surroundings as they covered each other when they went from room to room. All rooms except for one were unfurnished and empty. The room looking out over the back of the property was crammed full of mismatched pieces of furniture ranging from chairs, a bed, a dresser with one drawer missing, several boxes with football trophies, baseball mitts, as well as two old tennis rackets, and other junk.

Several boxes were stacked in one corner of the room. "Let's check what's in there. Could be files, data, stuff about the quantum computer."

Tiger nodded. "I'll take care of that. You should go back to the machine; figure out how to switch it off if we need to."

Dylan knew instantly why Tiger was concerned. During his first day at the mansion, Tiger and the others had recounted the incident when they'd tried to get Tiger out of the machine. It had taken them way too long to figure out how to switch off the machine, and as a result, Tiger had endured massive headaches for several weeks, though luckily there was no lasting damage to his brain.

"All right," Dylan agreed. "I'll check the machine."

He hurried downstairs. By now, he'd gotten used to the humming sound of the machine. It was merely white noise, and he was able to hear other sounds as well: a passing car, a dog barking outside. He looked at the computer screen to make himself familiar with the app that seemed to be running the MRI machine. He tapped on the mouse pad, but was unable to move the cursor, so he looked for an external mouse, but there was none. At the machine itself, a gurney stuck out of the circular part of the machine, ready to receive its next victim. But even there, he couldn't figure out how the gurney was operated. He tried to move it manually without success.

Dylan went around the machine, looking for a power cable, but to his surprise, there was none. Where was this machine getting its electricity from? He bent down to look underneath the MRI and used his cell phone light to illuminate the area. He saw it then: the power cable was beneath the machine, apparently plugged into a custom outlet on the ground—a truly unusual place to plug in such a device. Clearly, Polo had thought of everything. He didn't want anybody to disable his machine.

At a sound, Dylan turned, rising in the same instant. He froze when he saw who was entering the room through the door from the hallway: Zara. She wasn't alone, and she wasn't moving of her own will. Polo was holding a gun to her neck, his other hand clamped over her shoulder so she couldn't escape. Sheer fright was painted on her face, and he could only imagine what she was going through.

"Polo."

Polo grinned icily. The coldness in his eyes was the same as Dylan had seen in him over a decade earlier.

"I see no introductions are necessary. And what a surprise that you managed to turn one of my employees against me." He dipped his head to Zara's cheek then stared directly at him. "I must say, you almost got me. But I saw this in my premonition. I saw you and Zara come here."

That news wasn't entirely unexpected. After all, Polo had always been a step ahead of them. "So that's how you did it."

Polo chuckled. "My precognitive skills are so much more developed than yours. I'm superior to all of you. And you made it so easy for me. You left dear Zara here outside. Alone. Unprotected. That's on you, Hawk."

"Leave her out of this," Dylan said loudly, hoping that Tiger would eventually hear him over the din of the machine, because he'd just realized something: Polo hadn't mentioned Tiger. Had his vision not shown him that Tiger was here too? "She has nothing to do with this. It's me you want."

"You know as well as I do that I have no bargaining chip if I let her go now." He narrowed his eyes. "Don't play me for a fool. We both know I'm not."

"You sure about that?" He gestured to the machine. "Or do I have to remind you that my friends blew up your first machine not too long ago? And managed to save one of our own in the process?"

Polo scoffed. "And I'm actually grateful for that. It's given me the opportunity to upgrade the machine." He tipped his chin toward it. "Once a person is on the gurney, the sensors set everything in motion. Untearable belts lock the patient in place, and the gurney moves into the machine without anybody, not even myself, being able to pull it out until the program is finished. The sequence can't be overridden. Sorry."

His last word dripped with sarcasm. Polo didn't know the meaning of sorry. No psychopath did. It was a mere taunt, but Dylan didn't let it distract him. Instead, he made calculations in his head of how long it would take to push Zara away from her captor, before he could shoot her. The answer was: too long. There was no way to get to her in time. All he could do was stall. The situation made him feel more helpless than he'd ever felt. He didn't care what happened to him, whether Polo managed to hurt or kill him, but he couldn't allow anything to happen to Zara. She was an innocent.

"So this is your second machine, I see," Dylan said, raising his voice. "How many of us have you scanned already? Can't be enough, or you wouldn't still need the machine to feed your quantum computer. Must be tough to not live up to your own expectations."

The taunting words seemed to work, because Polo narrowed his eyes, glaring at him. "Don't you worry about me. Everything is running perfectly. In fact, once I have the data in your head, I won't need any more of your sort. Turns out that with each data set I feed into the computer the algorithm learns exponentially, much faster than I expected. So, I'm actually ahead of schedule."

It was obvious that Polo enjoyed talking about his own achievements.

"Congratulations," Dylan said, before finding another tidbit to keep him talking. "Tell me, your father didn't die a natural death, did he? You couldn't wait until heart disease or a stroke would have killed him in a few years. You needed to speed things up, didn't you?"

"Good old Dad never really understood me. But people who think they love you are so easy to manipulate. They trust you, and that makes them vulnerable." Polo shrugged. "It was his time anyway. He was turning into an old tattering fool. I did him a favor really."

"He was a good man," Zara suddenly choked out. "How could you?"

"You wouldn't understand," Polo snapped. "But enough of this. Let's get down to business." He jerked his chin toward the machine. "Hawk, if you will... I warmed the machine up for you. It's ready. And I'm getting impatient."

Dylan perceived a movement in the dark hallway behind Polo, though he couldn't be sure. "One last thing... a word of goodbye for Zara..."

Polo grunted.

He looked deep into Zara's eyes, wishing in that moment that his skill was that of telepathy, but he hoped she would understand anyway. "Zara... duck."

From behind Polo, Tiger emerged with a tennis racket that he swung toward Polo's left side, the impact making Polo sway to the right. The hand holding the gun made an uncoordinated movement, while Zara dove as low as she could. Dylan charged toward her. At the same time, Tiger landed another hit with the tennis racket that now broke into two, while Polo tumbled to the right and lost the grip on his gun. It clattered to the floor.

Dylan reached Zara and pulled her up, pushing her behind him in the next instant. "Get behind the machine."

It was the safest place in case Polo reached his gun and began shooting. Without looking behind him to see if Zara was following his command, he rushed toward Polo, who had already regained his balance and now kicked Tiger in the stomach to force him back toward the wall.

"Didn't see you coming," Polo ground out as he lunged for the gun.

Dylan tackled him, wrestling him to the ground, but Polo's hand was already wrapping around the butt of the gun. Dylan punched him, but Polo was surprisingly strong. A counterpunch hit him hard, and he fell backwards, giving Polo the upper hand.

Polo pointed the gun right at Dylan's chest, when Tiger rammed him from the side, this time hitting him so hard, that he lifted off his feet and landed on the gurney, the gun going off at the same time.

Zara screamed, and Dylan whipped his head in her direction. She stood close to the machine. He ran his eyes over her, scanning for injuries, but he saw none. Relieved, he let out a breath. With it, he felt a sharp pain sear through him. He looked down and saw blood seep from his upper arm, drenching his jacket. Polo had managed to shoot him. He lifted his arm, looked at both sides, and sighed with relief. The bullet had gone right through it.

There was another scream, this one from a man.

Dylan looked toward its origin. Polo was lying on the gurney. He was tied to it by firm belts. Tiger stood a few feet away, just looking at Polo, while he continued screaming.

"Get me the fuck out of here! Get me out!" Polo screamed at the top of his lungs.

Zara ran into his arms, and Dylan held her tightly. "Are you okay?"

She nodded, tears in her eyes. "You're hurt."

"It's nothing."

Tiger stepped closer to the MRI machine, looking down on Polo, while the machine continued humming and following its preset sequence, the gurney slowly rolling into the circular part of the machine.

"Help me! Get me out!"

Polo fought against his restraints, but the fear in his eyes confirmed that he'd spoken the truth earlier, when he'd said that once the sequence was initiated, it couldn't be overridden. He knew his fate was sealed.

Tiger bent over him. "Now you know what it feels like. See you on the other side."

The gurney with Polo on it disappeared in the machine, and the circular part of it began to spin around him, the tempo increasing with every second, while the computer monitor woke up and showed a screen that looked like a seismograph recording an earthquake.

Zara cast a glance at the machine, before turning back to Dylan. "We need to stop the bleeding."

By the time Zara had found medical supplies and bandaged his wound to stop the bleeding, the machine came to a stop and the gurney emerged. Polo lay there, not moving, his eyes open, staring into the void.

Dylan looked at the computer monitor that had now switched to a different window. He pointed to it. "What's that mean?"

Tiger looked at it and pointed to the various lines. "That's his current brain activity. And that's his heart rate and blood pressure."

"He's still alive?" Zara asked.

Tiger nodded. "Yes, he's got a heartbeat. But he's a vegetable. No brain activity."

Zara looked stunned.

Dylan squeezed her arm. "He deserved it. He killed a lot of people, and he would have killed even more."

She nodded. "I know. It's just hard to watch."

"What are we gonna do with the machine?" Tiger asked. "We can't just leave it here."

"We can't blow it up here," Dylan said, shaking his head.

"We're in the middle of D.C. There's no buffer zone between this building and its neighbors. Let's get everything we can carry: the server, the computers."

"Johnson dropped his briefcase in the hallway," Zara said. "The data discs have to be in there."

Tiger walked into the hallway and came back with a briefcase a moment later. He opened it, and nodded. "Yep, the data discs are here."

"Good, let's take those," Dylan said. "We'll discuss with Fox later how to best disable this machine. We might have to dismantle it, and transport it out of here piecemeal."

Tiger nodded. "It's a plan." Then he pointed to Polo. "What about him?"

"Zara, do you know his home address?" Dylan asked.

"Yes, why?"

"I have an idea."

28

———

Z ara topped off her wine glass and turned back to where all the residents of Ace's mansion crowded around the television in the kitchen. Dylan put his good arm around her waist and pulled her to his side. It was evening. Everybody had done their share today to make sure that nothing that had transpired in D.C. and the surrounding areas would lead back to them.

Fox and Michelle had worked on wiping all data related to the Stargate program from Polo's electronic devices, so that they could leave them in his condo. It had been necessary, because simply taking his computers and cell phone would have raised suspicion and indicated foul play once they found him. Meanwhile, Yankee, Ace, and Tiger had returned to the building where the MRI machine was located, and had dismantled it, then transported it away with a van disguised as a moving truck. Dylan had stayed at the mansion where Lilly had attended to his gunshot wound, confirming that no vital nerves or bones had been damaged, and the bullet had gone straight through him. He now wore his left arm in a sling.

"Turn it up," Yankee demanded, and a moment later, the newscaster's voice filled the room.

"...now have confirmation that a bomb was diffused earlier today at Joint Force Andrews following an anonymous tip. No terrorist organization has claimed responsibility for this attempted bombing of a military airport." The screen split, and in addition to the female reporter sitting in the studio, a camera feed showed a male reporter on the tarmac. *"Michael, have you spoken to officials at Joint Force Andrews to give us more information on what is behind this attack?"*

There was a brief pause, then the reporter spoke. *"Hello, Caroline, sources here at Joint Force Andrews are tightlipped. The bomb squad was called here mid-morning, shortly after the plane carrying the body of the VP's son arrived here. However, a military spokesman would not disclose where the bomb was located, and whether it could have killed the president and the VP, had they arrived here this morning. Nor would they speculate as to whether the downing of Marine One and the bomb at Andrews are connected."*

Caroline nodded. *"In a press briefing earlier today, the White House press secretary stated that the downing of Marine One is an ongoing investigation, and was unwilling to divulge any information on whether these incidents were connected. Let's talk to Tricia Black who's outside the Capitol building, which was evacuated earlier today. Tricia, what's the latest you can report?"*

The screen changed, and a woman standing in front of the Capitol appeared. Behind her, heavy security was protecting the building.

"Yes, Caroline, earlier today, the Capitol was evacuated after the bomb squad was called. Details are spotty, but several staffers I spoke to claimed that a bomb had been found on the House side of the Capitol building. While paramedics were called to the scene, no injuries other than minor scrapes that resulted from people

tripping and falling during the evacuation have been reported. For now, nobody has given any information as to who was the target of this bomb, which was successfully diffused. Over to you, Caroline."

"Thank you, Tricia." The screen filled with the newscaster again. *"We will follow the developments of these incidents. In other news from the Hill..."* A picture of Senator Johnson appeared in the top left corner of the screen. *"Senator James Johnson, the junior senator of Idaho, who was appointed to his father's seat only a month ago has suffered a massive stroke. A neighbor in his condo building here in D.C. was alerted by water dripping through the ceiling and notified the management company. They found Senator Johnson on the floor of his bathroom, his bath overflowing. It appears that he returned home after the Capitol was evacuated, and suffered a stroke in his condo, while running a bath. He's been transported to George Washington University Hospital, but according to a statement by the treating physician, the senator is in a vegetative state..."*

Ace turned down the volume. "It's done. They bought it. There'll be investigations, of course, but they'll never really figure out the truth." Then he motioned to Fox and Yankee. "The explosion of Bancroft's house didn't even make the news."

Fox grinned. "I won't take it personally. It was a busy news day."

Yankee shrugged. "I'm not looking for a trophy."

"It's really over?" Phoebe asked, her newborn baby in her arms.

Ace put his arm around the two, and kissed Phoebe on the forehead. "Yes, babe. It's finally over."

"So, what's next?" Dylan asked.

Ace grinned. "For starters, Phoebe is gonna make an honest man out of me, and you're all invited to the wedding."

Clapping and hollering filled the kitchen.

"I want to thank all of you for all the sacrifices you made, for the risks you took, for your friendship," Ace said, a wet sheen covering his irises, "for your loyalty, and your tenacity to pull this through. And for helping me get justice for my father." Ace lifted his glass. "To Henry Sheppard, for bringing us together."

"To Henry Sheppard," everybody called out and lifted their glass.

As they all—except for Phoebe—drank, Zara smiled at Dylan, and he leaned in and kissed her. From the corner of her eyes, she saw the other couples hugging and kissing too. They'd sacrificed so much of their private lives for much longer than she had. She could hear them talking, making plans for the future.

"I'm gonna have to find a job," Yankee said.

"Me too," Tiger added. "Not sure what I can get with my qualifications as ex-CIA agent and Yoga teacher. Any suggestions?"

"I'm sure our skills are useful in many jobs..." Dylan mused. "Risk management? Private Investigations?" He shrugged. "I don't know." He motioned to Ace. "Maybe Ace wants to open up an outfit where we could all use our precognitive skills..."

Everybody laughed.

"I think the first thing I'll do," Ace announced, "is to take a long vacation with the two people I love most in this world." He smiled at Phoebe and their son, before he looked back at the assembled. "We'll see about the future later. I have to figure out first what I really want in this life, now that I have choices again."

At those words, Zara locked eyes with Dylan. They had choices too. One was a simple one, at least for her. "I guess we can now move to my place, can't we?"

"You want me to move in with you?"

"Don't you want to?"

"I do." He pulled her into his arms and kissed her softly.

29

Dylan rummaged through his belongings that fit into two travel bags, which now stood next to the closet in Zara's bedroom, until he'd found what he was looking for. His left arm still hurt like hell, and it would take a few weeks to fully heal, but Lilly had given him painkillers for it, which he was grateful for.

"I have nothing edible in the fridge," Zara called from the hallway.

They'd left Ace's mansion only an hour earlier with the promise to stay in touch, a promise Dylan would keep. The other four ex-Stargate agents were like brothers to him now.

Zara popped her head into the bedroom. "Unpack later. Let's go get something to eat."

Dylan turned and rose, the item he'd been looking for concealed in his right hand. He smiled at Zara. "I just need to do one thing before we go."

He motioned her to come closer. With a furrowed forehead, Zara approached. "Do what?"

"What I should have done four years ago." He opened his palm, revealing the diamond ring he'd carried with him for four long years. "Will you marry me, Zara?"

Zara slapped both hands over her mouth. "Oh my God!" Tears welled up in her eyes.

"Did you really think I'd just move in without fully committing to you?" He shook his head. "I was a fool to leave you back then."

"Dylan, I don't even know what to say…" She reached for him.

"It's simple. Say yes." He took her hand and slipped the ring on her finger.

A tear loosened from one eye and ran down her cheek. "Yes, Dylan, yes."

He drowned out her answer with a kiss and pulled her close. When she pressed her body to his, pain seared through his biceps, and he winced and pulled back.

"I'm so sorry, Dylan," she said. "I shouldn't have hugged you so hard."

He chuckled despite the pain. "You can hug me as hard as you want." He put his right arm around her waist, and dipped his head to hers again. "Are you very hungry?"

Awareness flickered in her eyes. "I'll survive if we don't get food right away."

"Good. I was hoping you'd say that. 'Cause I want to make love to you."

"What about your injury?"

"Forget about my arm. There's nothing wrong with my cock."

Zara slid her hand over the bulge in his pants. "Yeah, I can feel that. How about I help you undress?"

"I'd appreciate it."

Zara undressed him as expertly as was possible with his arm in the sling. He had no other choice but to get his left arm out of it, so it wouldn't be in their way. He lowered himself on the bed, while Zara peeled off layer after layer of her own clothing, treating him to a striptease that made his cock even harder. And more impatient.

"Now you're just teasing me," he said with a smirk.

"That's the idea," she confessed and approached the bed.

She ran her eyes over him and licked her lips, before she lowered herself onto the bed, pushing his thighs apart to make space for herself there.

"Fuck!"

Zara greeted his curse with a smirk. "I thought I'd nurse you back to health..."

She licked her tongue over the crown of his erection, sending a bolt akin to an electrical shock through his body. Another curse burst from his lips.

"Fuck, baby! You're gonna kill me!"

"I doubt that," she murmured. "I remember all too well how much you always enjoyed me taking your big cock into my mouth."

She had the audacity to look at him with her lips pursed in mock-innocence. He sat up and put his hand on her nape, making her lift her head further. "Damn it, Zara, don't torture me." He kissed her hard, before he released her lips again.

Zara pressed him back into the sheets. "Now be good, and let me suck you."

A second later, Zara's lips wrapped around the tip of his cock, and she took him deep into her mouth. At the tantalizing sensation of wet heat engulfing his hard-on, a shudder raced down his spine, and a moan loosened from his lips. He was in heaven. All other thoughts and worries, even the pain of his injury fell away, and what was left was the knowledge that Zara still loved him the way she had four years ago. He didn't know why he'd gotten so lucky to have her in his life again, but he didn't question it any further. They belonged together.

"I love you, Zara," he murmured and reached for her face, making her lift her head. His cock slipped from her mouth. "Ride me, baby."

She mounted him, impaling herself on his erection. "I love you, Dylan."

She began to ride him just like he remembered, first slowly in a measured tempo, then faster and harder.

He pulled her face down to his. "This time it's forever."

When he took her lips in a passionate kiss, he could finally see it: the future they would have. A life full of love, and joy, and laughter. The life they'd earned.

ABOUT THE AUTHOR

Tina Folsom was born in Germany and has been living in English speaking countries since 1991. Tina has always been a bit of a globe trotter.

She lived in Munich, Lausanne, London, New York City, Los Angeles, San Francisco, and Sacramento. She has now made a beach town in Southern California her permanent home with her American husband and her dog.

She's written over 50 romance novels in English most of which are translated into German, French, and Spanish.

https://tinafolsom.com
tina@tinafolsom.com

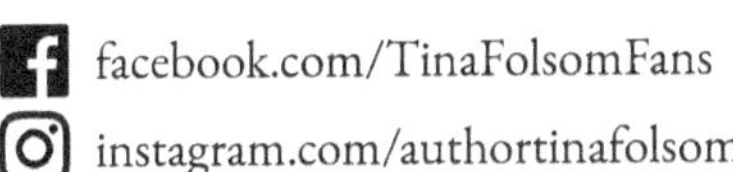

facebook.com/TinaFolsomFans
instagram.com/authortinafolsom

www.ingramcontent.com/pod-product-compliance
Lightning Source LLC
Chambersburg PA
CBHW021551310726
48972CB00003B/771